MIDNIGHT COWBOYS

Midnight Rodeo
Two Cowboys for Christie
Three for the Rodeo

Luxie Ryder

MENAGE AMOUR

Siren Publishing, Inc.
www.SirenPublishing.com

A SIREN PUBLISHING BOOK
IMPRINT: Ménage Amour

MIDNIGHT COWBOYS
Midnight Rodeo
Two Cowboys for Christie
Three for the Rodeo
Copyright © 2009 by Luxie Ryder

ISBN-10: 1-60601-140-5
ISBN-13: 978-1-60601-140-9

First Printing: October 2009

Cover design by Jinger Heaston
All cover art and logo copyright © 2009 by Siren Publishing, Inc.

Printed in the U.S.A.

PUBLISHER
Siren Publishing, Inc.
www.SirenPublishing.com

DEDICATION

Midnight Rodeo
To my sister – fighting the biggest challenge of her life. You make
me very proud.

Two Cowboys for Christie
To my fiancé who will have become my husband by the time this
book is released. Nothing else matters…

Luxie Ryder

Siren Publishing

Ménage Amour

MIDNIGHT RODEO

LUXIE RYDER

MIDNIGHT RODEO
Midnight Cowboys 1

LUXIE RYDER

Chapter 1

'A couple more beers over here, darlin'.'

Talia bit down a snappy retort. The cowboys at the end of the bar had been calling her names all night, albeit affectionate ones and it was beginning to wear on her nerves. She'd told them what she liked to be called with a tight smile more than once, but they seemed determined not to use it.

'There ya go.' She placed the drinks in front of the two men, one as dark as the other was fair.

'Thanks, sweetheart,' the blonde one said.

'The name is Talia,' she repeated through gritted teeth as she walked away to get their change. By the time she returned, two pairs of eyes were anticipating her arrival.

'I guess we're bugging you?' The darker one smiled, dimples appearing in his unshaven face. 'We really don't mean to, it's just that we meet so many people out on the road, we tend to forget they have names.'

Talia smiled back, remembering that it wasn't their fault she was so irritated. Since the Rodeo and Wild West Show had arrived in Chelwood the day before, her little bar had been insanely busy. One of the staff had called in sick too, leaving her to cope with the evening shift alone.

The lighter of the two men stood, taking off his hat. 'My name is Reb. This here is Cody. Pleased to make your acquaintance, Ma'am.' His friend got to his feet briefly, tipping his head in greeting. Both men looked to be in their mid- thirties and stood a little over six feet, towering over her by about ten inches. They were dressed alike in t-shirts and jeans along with their hats, but that is where any similarities ended. Reb had a long, rangy body made brown from too many hours in the sun and an easy smile he seemed to have trouble keeping under control. Cody was paler but still very tan with a strong, broad frame and penetrating dark eyes.

'So, what do you think of our little piece of Colorado?' Talia asked, trying to move the conversation forward and divert their attention from the fact she'd been such a grouch. A couple guys further down the bar were hollering for more beer, but she ignored them.

'Beautiful,' they said, almost in unison.

'You own this place?' Cody asked, gesturing toward the rest of the building.

Talia nodded. 'I inherited The Watering Hole from my father when he decided to retire and take my mother back home to Mexico.'

'Well, you are doing a fine job,' smiled Reb. 'It looks great.'

'Thanks,' she smiled as she turned away to grab a couple more bottles from the cooler. 'Here, these are on the house,' she said, feeling the need to make amends. Cody's watchful gaze was still on her body as she turned and he showed no embarrassment or remorse when he realized she'd caught him.

'Thank you—Talia,' he said, allowing his eyes to linger on her as he took a long swallow of his beer. His gaze went through her, causing a tightening between her legs that she was almost sure he could see.

Damn! She wanted what he was selling. Talia knew her reaction to the sexy cowboy was caused almost entirely by a self imposed sexual drought. Her crotch got moist at the invitation in his eyes and the sensation increased as she watched his tongue lick a stray bead of beer from his lip. Things were far worse than she'd realized if a handsome stranger could make her so hot without even trying.

She dragged her gaze away, moving back down the bar; sure she could still feel his eyes on her. She'd been told many times that her ass was her best feature and she got a lot of comments on it. Men seemed to like her long legs and small tight butt. Personally, Talia felt she was a little too skinny, but she did like her long, black hair. Her features, like her name, came from her mother's Mexican heritage.

Despite her aroused state, Reb and Cody were the last things on her mind for the next hour or so. The bar filled to capacity, forcing her to shout over the noise of the chatter to hear what the customers wanted. A small crowd at the other end of the room was beginning to get rowdy, shouting for more beer constantly as they laughed and hollered to their buddies.

'Hang on,' she yelled back as they called for service again. A sudden movement behind her caught her eye and she turned just in time to see Reb running passed toward the end of the galley. Next thing anyone knew, the young reveler who had jumped the counter to grab some free drinks for his buddies, found himself being thrown back over the bar to land in a heap on top of his friends.

The guy regained his balance and took a step forward, ready to retaliate. 'I wouldn't if I were you.' A strong hand held him back by the shoulder as Cody appeared behind him as if from nowhere. The kid thought better of it, shrugging off the restraining touch and storming from the building, followed by his friends.

'Sorry about that,' Reb said as he squeezed passed Talia on his way back to his seat on the other side of the bar. 'Looked like you could use a hand.'

'Yeah, thanks,' she said, a little taken aback by the turn of events and the casual ease with which he had touched her, seemingly unmoved by the full body contact. Talia could still feel his hands on her hips. The earlier arousal caused by Cody slammed through her anew.

Cody retook his seat, slapping Reb on the back with a laugh. 'Can you warn me next time?'

'I knew you'd be right behind me,' he said.

Cody turned to her. 'You want us to watch the door? In case that guy wants back in?'

Talia began to shake her head before looking around and realizing she was hopelessly overwhelmed. 'I could use a little help,' she smiled, 'but I pay my way. Your drinks are on me, ok?'

Closing time came with no further incidents. True to their word, the guys kept an eye on the crowd, shutting anything down before it could escalate and limiting the amount of people through the door.

Talia's attention returned to them fully as the last few stragglers fell out into the night. They'd come back to sit at the bar about an hour earlier as the crowd had begun to thin out. Every time she'd looked their way, they'd been looking at her. A couple times she was sure she caught them talking about her, but she had no way to be sure.

'Another beer guys?' she offered.

'Only if you join us,' Reb said, making a space between him and his buddy. Talia locked the door then sat down nervously.

'Thanks so much for your help. I don't know how I would have coped without you both.'

'Not a problem,' said Cody.

'Don't mention it,' said Reb.

'So, are you guys with the rodeo?' she asked.

'I just take care of the horses,' Reb replied, nodding towards his friend. 'Cody here is the superstar.'

'You're a rider? Isn't that a little dangerous?'

He nodded. 'Can be. You just gotta take precautions.'

'Sounds like an exciting life, travelling from town to town. Have you done it long?' she asked, unnerved by the way both men had turned toward her, each placing an arm along the back of her chair as their knees bumped with hers.

'Me and Reb have been working together about ten years,' Cody answered.

Reb nodded his agreement. 'We're like an old married couple,' he laughed. 'Eating, sleeping, partying—you name it, Cody is always right there with me. Get sick of the sight of him sometimes.' Mirth twinkled in his light green eyes as he teased his friend.

'You do everything together?'

'Everything,' Cody said after a pause, staring into her eyes. Talia heard Reb laugh as he took a pull on his beer and she stared from one to the other, wondering what it was she had missed that was so funny.

'Ok, well thanks again,' she said, trying to make it clear she was waiting to close up.

She wriggled to her feet, barely able to get out of her seat with the two large men trapping her between them. 'Excuse me,' she said to Cody, gesturing that she wanted to get passed.

He took his time getting up but he moved out of her way, smiling as she hid her eyes when she got level with him. 'Thanks,' she mumbled.

'Don't mention it.'

Talia hovered next to them, unsure why Cody continued to stare at her so intently. The tension was broken when he turned to his friend and patted him on the shoulder. 'Come on, buddy, the lady wants us out of here.'

Reb drained the last of his beer, smacking his lips in appreciation as he got to his feet. 'Thanks for the free drinks,' he smiled warmly.

'It was the least I could do,' she said, moving toward the door in the hope they would follow. 'I really appreciated your help.'

'Cody's a sucker for a maiden in distress,' he teased, elbowing his friend in the ribs and ignoring the dark look he got in return.

'Well, I'm grateful there are still some gentlemen around.' Both of them seemed to preen a little at the compliment, making her smile. Men were so easy to please.

'Are you coming to the rodeo?' Cody asked, seeming reluctant to walk through the door she was now holding open for them. He pressed a ticket into her hand after she shook her head. 'Drop by and see us if you get the time.'

Talia promised she would, mostly due the fact Reb scooped her against his hard body and wouldn't let her go until she did. 'Put her down, Reb,' Cody said, taking his hat off to kiss her cheek as he finally left the bar. His friend did the same on her other side, trailing a casual hand over her hip as he strolled out of the door.

Talia slid the bolt home before turning to lean back against the wood, releasing a shaky breath. She'd handled many a horny cowboy in her twenty nine years, but never two at the same time.

They both seemed aware of the other's attraction to her and neither seemed to mind. She wondered what would have happened if she'd encouraged one of them over the other?

Chapter 2

Talia spotted the pair of them the next afternoon as she approached the rough stock ring. Reb was barely visible inside the chute as he worked on the horse Cody sat on.

She took a seat in the stand, feeling the adrenalin from the ring below seep into her. The noise was immense as impatient horses and indignant cattle making their voices heard, competing for volume with the announcer shouting into a microphone.

Reb looked her way and stopped what he was doing to give her a wave, directing Cody's gaze toward her by poking him in the thigh. She saw him scanning the crowd for her so she waved nervously, hearing the murmurs of the people around her as the rider removed his hat and waved back at her with it. Talia looked around nervously; hoping that nobody had seen her flirting with some guys from the rodeo or could tell that she had spent much of the previous night masturbating at the thought of having them—both together and individually.

Ignoring the answering throb in her groin, she took a baseball cap from her large purse, and pulled the brim down over her eyes to shield them from the bright afternoon sun. The horse Cody rode seemed to be getting skittish, kicking at the sides of the stall as if trying to get out.

She saw Reb leap to the side, clambering out of the way moments before the chute gate opened. Cody's horse leapt forward, kicking his legs out even before he was clear of the bars.

Cody clung on, one hand threaded through a taut rope, his body jerking around in the saddle as he tried to stay on top of the bucking horse. She could see the concentration on his face and the way the muscles of his thighs contracted as he tightened them around the animal.

Talia couldn't tear her eyes away, despite being sure Cody would fall and be trampled at any moment. The noise of the announcer became a muffled distraction and she stood in her seat to get a better view, screaming a little as the horse finally won, unseating his tormentor before lashing out at him with an angry kick.

She covered her eyes then as she waited for the screams of the spectators, but they never came. Peeping through her fingers, she found Cody on his feet, brushing the dust from his chaps with his hat as he waved at the crowd. Turning her way, he gave her a deep bow, before laughing at her still shocked expression.

Talia dropped her hands, smiling back in relief as she saw the exhilaration on his face. He seemed to glow with excitement and she got a brief insight into why he would put himself in so much danger.

Cody gestured over his shoulder, using his arm to give her directions out of the stand and around to the side, inviting her to come down and join them. A few of the other young women in the crowd started giggling with excitement; sure the invitation included them, too.

By the time Talia reached the spot she'd been directed to, she was at the back of a very long line of people—men, women and children among them—all waiting for autographs or asking for photos.

Cody had clambered up onto the railings, taking the items handed up to him by Reb, signing them quickly and handing them back. He spotted Talia at the back of the throng and smiled, shrugging his shoulders in apology. Reb turned her way after a kick in the ribs, looking as if he meant to come get her until a kid thrust a camera into his hand and asked him to take a picture.

Talia waited as long as she could without feeling like a groupie herself. Pride eventually forced her to walk away once she realized she had no idea why she was actually waiting to see them. A loud whistle made her turn around and she saw Cody raise his hands as if asking where she was going.

She pointed at her watch, trying to tell him she had to get back to work. Cody nodded that he understood and then mimed drinking a bottle of beer and gave her the thumbs up when she got what he was saying. They would drop by and see her later.

Despite her excuses to Cody, Talia didn't go straight back to work, taking her time instead to walk through the fair. Years had passed since she'd allowed herself some real time off and she was in no hurry to get back to the dark, lonely bar.

Settling down in the shade of a large oak, she kicked off her shoes and leaned back against the trunk, resolving to enjoy the giant candy floss she'd just bought.

She was regretting the decision a few minutes later as the sticky sweet fluff clung to her fingers, refusing to come unstuck. Talia could feel some on her chin and tried to wipe it away with the back of a hand, realizing too late that she'd dragged the candy floss across her hair in the process.

About to get up and toss it in the trash so she could free herself up from the pink hell she was in, she stopped when two large shadows blocked out the sun. Cody and Reb looked down at her, suppressed laughter making the corners of their mouths twitch as their eyes roved over her hands, face and hair.

'Don't just stand there, help me,' she said, laughing as they both put a hand under her armpits and dragged her to her feet.

Chapter 3

They were still laughing at her as they walked into her bar again later that night. 'If you wanted to be covered in candy floss, you only had to let us know,' Reb teased. 'We'd be happy to oblige.'

'Oh God, don't remind me,' she groaned, face a little flushed as she remembered what she'd looked like when she got home. The light pink fluff had begun to dry out, turning a bright red. Talia had been forced to scrub her hands, her chin and the tip of her nose to get the color out of them before washing her hair twice. 'What the hell do they make that stuff out of?' she asked on a laugh.

'Nuclear waste,' Cody drawled, smiling as she slapped him on the arm.

Talia got them both a beer before leaving them to each other's company as she focused her attention on the growing crowd. At least she had some help tonight, she thought as Cindy rushed in through the door, apologizing for being late.

As the night wore on, Talia got the distinct impression that Cody and Reb were waiting until she was free to get another round of drinks. Cindy had been hovering all night, her pretty blonde face lighting up hopefully every time they looked her way.

'It's not fair.' She pouted later, cornering Talia by the till. 'I been flirting my ass off all night long and neither of those dudes at the end of the bar are taking a blind bit of notice.'

'I guess they're just here to drink, that's all,' Talia offered, knowing from her own experience that it wasn't true. Tonight, as they had been the night before, Cody and Reb were watching her constantly. And their eyes had rarely been on her face.

At first, she'd smiled back at them each time she found they were looking her way. Eventually, she'd tried to ignore them, feeling the skin on whatever body part they were staring at start to tingle as she noticed their eyes on her again. Talia was no longer in any doubt that they were talking about her intimately.

'Talia,'

She walked toward Cody, stopping on the way to grab a couple more bottles, assuming it was why they were calling her. Her nipples contracted painfully as the cold air from the chiller blasted them, her body already sensitized from the heat building inside her.

Any hopes she had that they hadn't noticed flew out of the window when she saw Reb's hand freeze in mid air, his bottle half way to his lips. He gathered his wits as she got nearer, finally taking a slug on his beer, but unable to drag his eyes away from her.

'I wasn't asking for more beer,' he said, voice sounding a little hoarse. 'But thanks.'

'Oh, sorry, what was it you wanted?' she asked innocently, regretting her choice of words as she watched him bite back a retort. If the expression on his face was anything to go by, he'd been about to tell her in no uncertain terms, but thought better of it.

His eyes dropped to her chest for the briefest moment before he hid them under the brim of his hat, gesturing over his shoulder with a nod of his head. 'That jerk from last night just walked in. Do you want us to get rid of him?'

Talia scanned the room, spotting the small group in a corner. 'If you can do it without causing a scene, I'd appreciate it,' she said, deciding that the kid and his friend's money weren't worth the risk of the damage they could do if a fight broke out.

Reb was off his chair before Talia finished speaking, walking toward the young men with his arms outstretched, guiding the group in the direction of the door. Talia could hear a few of them cursing before one stepped forward, about to square up to Reb. She turned to alert Cody, only to find he'd already moved, crossing the room to stand firmly in front of the trouble maker as if daring him to make a move.

The kid dropped his gaze, turning around and walking back out, shouting over his shoulder that the place was a dump anyway. Reb went to follow him out of the door until Cody held him back with a strong hand. 'The lady said not to cause a scene,' he reminded him, patting him on the shoulder as he saw the tension ease out of him.

'I guess I owe you another drink,' she offered as they retook their seats.

Reb shook his head, fixing his green eyes on hers, unusually serious for a moment. 'You can pay us back later,' he said mysteriously, holding her gaze.

Talia fought the urge to groan aloud, walking away from the intense heat emanating from the two men, almost breathless from the burning throb between her thighs. *What the hell were they trying to do to her?*

Cindy went home an hour later, taking her time gathering her things as she realized the cowboys intended to stay a while longer, finally leaving Talia alone with them.

'I'm starving,' Cody said, dragging her attention back to them and away from loading the glasses into the dishwasher. 'Is there anywhere to eat around here?'

Talia smiled. 'Not a chance at this time of night. Welcome to small town USA.'

'I'm so hungry, I could eat my hat.' Reb laughed, winking at her as he dropped a hint as big as a boulder.

Despite the late hour and how tired she was, Talia knew the only polite thing to do after they'd been so helpful was to at least offer them a meal. 'I can rustle something up,' she offered.

'Are you sure you don't mind?' Cody said, relief flooding his face.

'Of course not. Give me a minute to shut up properly and we can go through to the kitchen.' She slipped from the room, relieved to be out of the highly charged situation for a moment.

'Damn, that was good,' Reb exclaimed ten minutes later after wolfing down the burger she'd prepared.

'Do you want some more?' Talia asked.

'No, that was more than enough,' Cody answered, giving Reb a look that dared him to continue nodding his head. 'Thanks.'

She felt his smile right down to her toes, beginning to blush. 'No problem.'

'So, do you live here?' Reb asked, placing his elbows on the table.

Talia nodded. 'I have an apartment upstairs.'

'What does your guy think about you working so late?' Cody said.

'There is no guy,' she said, feeling defensive. 'It's just me and my cat.'

Reb and Cody looked at each other again, an unspoken conversation passing between them.

'You and the cat?' Was Reb laughing at her?

'Yes. Is it that hard to believe?'

Cody interrupted. 'What he means is it's hard to imagine a pretty thing like you living all alone.'

'Not so hard if you knew my ex.' She laughed, unwilling to explain that hell would freeze over before she let a man into her life again. Well, at least not any time soon.

Again, the conversation died, leaving her sitting between the men. Both of them seemed content to simply stare at her as if enjoying her discomfort. 'I usually have a hot drink before I turn in for the night, do you want one before you leave?' she hinted, hoping they realized they couldn't stay in her kitchen much longer.

'Yes, please,' Reb said, getting to his feet. 'I'll be right back, gotta visit the head.' He smiled, walking from the room.

'Cody?' He hadn't answered her, just continued to stare into her eyes. 'Are you having a drink?'

He nodded, getting to his feet to stand beside her. 'Here, let me get that,' he offered as she reached above her head for the cookie jar. His body bumped hers gently and he grasped her hips to hold her steady. Talia put down the jar, unnerved by his nearness and the fact he still hadn't let go of her. She swallowed hard as she realized he intended to kiss her.

Cody's lips met hers as she stared up at him mutely. Her body reacted as her brain warned it not to, and she found herself returning the kiss, not stopping him as his hands dropped down to cup her ass. 'I've been dying to touch this all night,' he mumbled against her mouth as he pulled her closer, pressing his hard cock into her.

Talia raised her hands to push him away, but instead, clutched the fabric of his t-shirt, pulling him nearer. She'd wanted to touch him since he'd first made her wet and she didn't allow herself time to question what was happening.

Cody slid a hand up to her torso, chuckling in the back of his throat as he allowed his palm to brush over her taut nipple before closing over her breast. Talia groaned at the contact, feeling a pulse begin in her pussy. He wrapped his free hand in her hair, tugging her head backward gently to allow him to bite into her neck before bringing his mouth back to hers.

Talia felt another body press into her back. Jumping away in surprise, she found Reb staring down at her, lust making his eyes seem darker. The boyish grin had been chased away by a look of intense concentration. 'W…what are you doing?' she asked, surprised by Cody's lack of reaction to the interruption.

'I told you we do everything together…'

Chapter 4

Reb smiled, smoothing a finger over her cheek before allowing it to trail down to the nipple poking through her top.

'Whoa, guys. I don't know if I can do this,' she said, taking a step back. Cody wrapped a hand around her wrist gently, stopping her flight.

'Why not?'

'Why not?' she repeated feeling cornered. 'Well, I barely know you for a start.'

'We both want you, Talia,' Reb said, running a hand down her other arm. 'We've been watching you all night,' he breathed, pulling her closer, 'watching your lovely dark hair brush over your body and that sexy little ass swaying back and forth under our noses.'

'And we know you want us,' Cody said, sliding his hand across the small of her back, urging her closer. 'I saw the way you looked at me earlier and how you reacted when Reb touched you. Your nipples got hard instantly, just like they are now.'

Talia laughed nervously. 'Look, guys. It's not that I don't find the idea appealing—but it's just not my kind of thing, ok?'

'Why, because you're a good girl?' Reb teased, running a hand over her ass. 'Or is it because you are afraid people will find out.'

'A bit of both,' she said, her resolve starting to weaken as the men pulled her between them, pressing her forward into Cody's body as Reb slotted his behind. Her head began to spin as they continued to persuade her, taking turns to speak.

'It's ok to be a bad girl if you want to be, Talia,' Cody said, bunching her hair to one side to mutter hotly into her ear. 'Nobody will ever know.'

'Let us make you feel good,' Reb whispered, rubbing his erection against her ass as he moved closer. 'You know we can.'

'Don't be scared to take what you want,' Cody said, as she stared at him uncertainly. 'But if you want us to leave, just say so.' Both of the men froze, their heated breath wafting over her face and neck as they waited for her reply. 'Do you want us to leave Talia?'

The blood rushed in her ears as her heart skipped a beat at the prospect of the pleasure that could lie ahead if she could just reach out and grab it. She dropped Cody's gaze, shaking her head. 'No, I don't want you to leave.'

'You won't be sorry, baby,' Reb said, allowing his hand to slide between her legs. 'Fuck, Cody, she is so hot and wet I can feel it through her jeans.' He gasped, sinking his teeth into her shoulder. Talia's legs shook as Cody grasped both of her breasts, biting down gently at her lip as he sucked it into his mouth.

'Where's the bedroom?' He groaned, forcing himself to end the kiss. Talia whispered her answer, barely able to find her voice.

Reb walked away without warning, as if knowing that Cody would follow. Talia was scooped into the larger man's arms, and placed on the bed mere moments later. By the time she and Cody had reached the small room, Reb had discarded most of his clothing. He pulled her to her feet instantly to begin taking her t-shirt off as Cody quickly disrobed and then started on her jeans.

Both men stroked and kissed at each inch of skin they exposed, dropping onto their knees on either side of her as they helped her out of her trousers and panties. Reb stood behind her to unclasp her bra, kissing the skin of her back. Cody remained on his knees, sliding his eyes and his hands over her body, slipping his fingertips under the cups of her bra to caress her nipples.

'Fuck man, your body is beautiful,' Cody said.

'I told you it would be,' Reb replied over her shoulder, brushing Cody's hands out of the way as he filled his hands with her breasts.

Talia let her head fall back on Reb's shoulder as she watched Cody parting the curls at her groin. 'Oh God, I can see how wet you are,' he gasped, staring at her for a moment before running a finger over her swollen clit. She bucked, falling harder against Reb as Cody lowered his head, flicking his tongue over her. 'You taste so fucking sweet, baby.' He lifted her legs from the floor and placed them over his shoulders.

Reb held her firm, stepping back to increase the angle as she lay suspended between the two men.

'Hey, I wanna see,' Reb complained until Cody helped him lift her onto the bed, parting her legs for his friend. He groaned as he took over the task of teasing her clitoris, adding a finger to her torture as it slipped easily inside. Cody had moved to lie at her side, caressing her body as his warm lips kissed hers.

Talia didn't know where to focus her attention. The tightening in her pussy was no more due to what Reb was doing than it was to the sensation of Cody's mouth on hers and his fingers on her breasts. She reached down to where she could feel his erection bumping against her thigh and wrapped her small hand around it. Her thumb caressed the top, finding it wet with his arousal.

'Yes,' Cody said at her touch, thrusting gently into her palm. His large hand closed around her throat, holding her head firm as he deepened the onslaught of his mouth on hers.

Reb groaned against her skin as her pussy began to quiver a warning around his fingers. 'That's it, baby,' he said against her, increasing the pressure of his mouth. 'Let it go.'

Cody's tongue began to plunder her mouth, mimicking the action of Reb's. Talia started to come, biting down on Cody's lip until he pulled away to watch as her head fell back and she began to moan and shake beneath him.

'When Reb's done, I am gonna fuck you so hard you will scream,' he whispered into her ear, making a new wave of electricity spear through her at his words.

Reb kissed her thigh, crawling up the bed to lie beside her as Cody made his way down. 'Turn over,' he ordered, guiding her movements with a strong hand at her hip. Talia did as she was told, her body feeling heavy. On her knees, she began to quiver anew as she felt the tip of Cody's cock begin to push inside her cunt just as Reb came to kneel in front of her, inviting her to take his penis into her mouth.

She flicked her tongue over the head, careful not to have him in her mouth as she anticipated Cody's first, devastating thrust. He didn't disappoint, almost lifting her from the bed as he rammed his cock home. Talia gasped, letting her head drop in euphoria as wave after wave of sensation began to ripple through her, caused by the man filling her pussy.

Reb gave her a gentle reminder that he was waiting by lifting her chin, smiling at her with heavy lidded eyes and biting down on his lip as she opened her mouth and let him in. Cupping a fist halfway down his shaft, Talia allowed the pounding of her body to determine the speed and depth of her sucking, closing her lips around Reb's cock as Cody pulled her back, ready to accept his next thrust.

'How does her pussy feel?' Reb asked, voice breaking as she worked on him.

'Amazing man - fucking amazing,' Cody said, sounding near his peak.

'Ah, you've got a sweet mouth, baby,' Reb said, running a caressing hand down her face to hold her chin steady. 'I can't hold out much longer.'

'She's gonna come again,' Cody warned. 'I can feel her cunt sucking on me.' He reached under her hip, dropping a hand to her clitoris, biting the flesh on her back as he felt her reaction to his touch.

Reb bunched her hair in his hands, piling it on top of her head as he increased the speed of his thrusts into her mouth. 'Fuck...I'm coming,' he moaned, his thighs beginning to tremble as she removed her mouth and began to pump him frantically. Reb fell back against the wall, legs splayed, abdomen trembling as his semen pulsed onto his thigh, his gasps filling the air.

Talia felt Cody's reaction to Reb's orgasm—the hand at her clit rubbing her briskly as his fucking began to lift her body from the bed. Reb looked up from his stupor, smiling as he saw how near she was. Pulling her head onto the bed between his knees, he leaned over her back. Reb scooped her breasts into his hands, squeezing and pulling at her nipples as he rained kisses along her spine. 'Better give him what he wants,' she heard him say. 'Cody won't stop till he makes you explode.'

Talia sank her teeth into his thigh, gripping the flesh as she began to come. Reb used the hands on her breasts to hold her still as she instinctively pulled away from the source of a pleasure she could not bear. Her loud cries echoed off the walls, not quite a scream, but the sounds of a woman experiencing about as much as she could take. Cody's fingers and thrusts became more and more erratic until he followed her orgasm with his own.

She heard him growl in his throat, body jerking into hers, the way his cock slammed into her again and again almost painful until finally he fell away, releasing her.

For the first ten minutes after it ended, Talia could do no more than lay where they'd left her, panting and sweating. Eventually, muscles began to protest and the urge to move was unbearable. The moment she lifted her head, the men made way for her, clearing a gap in the center of the bed, and encouraging her to lie between them.

She lay on her front, feeling exposed without the cover of lust to chase away her inhibitions. Reb rolled onto his side, turning away after kissing her cheek. Cody caressed the skin on her back, tracing idle circles with his fingers and smoothing her hair.

The last thing she remembered before she fell asleep was Cody whispering into her ear. 'I didn't want to share.'

Chapter 5

Talia woke in the cold light of day, relieved to find she was alone. The two men must have left sometime in the night. Someone had covered her with the blanket and drawn the blinds, too.

She rolled onto her back, giggling like a naughty kid as she remembered what had happened the night before. The memory caused a small spear of desire to trickle through her, chasing away any embarrassment. She threw back the covers as she spied the clock, realizing she'd slept much too late. Her thighs, back and shoulders screamed in protest, making her pause. Talia laughed as she got up carefully. She'd forgotten what a night of lovemaking could do to you.

Feeling more human after her shower, she got down to work on the bar. Cleaning away the plates and cups from the kitchen brought back a memory, making her smile. Knowing she would spend all day catching up but not caring, she took her coffee over to the table, giggling once more as she sipped the fortifying brew.

She couldn't feel sorry or ashamed over what had happened. Two horny cowboys had devastated her, shaking any beliefs she'd had that she was a 'good girl'. The memory brought back Cody's words— including the last thing he'd said before she had fallen asleep. What had he meant?

As the day progressed, she caught herself smiling secretly every time she remembered the previous night. Certain parts kept playing over and over in her mind, like some old movie. Most of them involved Cody.

Customers began to drift in to the bar in the late afternoon and she resented their presence. She wanted to be left alone to reminisce; sure she would never experience anything so unique again. But as is so often the case, real life got in the way, and it was almost closing time before she thought of her lovers again.

'I'm just closing up,' she called over a shoulder as she heard footfalls crossing the floor of the bar.

'I sure hope not,' Reb drawled, smiling broadly as she turned around.

Cody rolled his eyes at the corny line. 'Is it ok that we are here?' Talia nodded with a shy smile, knowing he was asking so much more.

The night was a carbon copy of the one before, save for one important detail—Talia called the shots. By the time Cody dropped to his knees in exhaustion and Reb rolled away from her later that night, she'd demanded they'd take her in every way, while denying their satisfaction until the last moment.

She'd gotten away with it for a long time too; she smiled, as she thought back on it after they'd left. At least until Cody's frustration had shifted the balance of power.

Talia had relished the control she'd discovered she had over them, at one point leaving them standing over her, sweat coursing from their heaving bodies as she forced them to watch her masturbate. Cody had kept his distance, eyes warning her that she would pay for such teasing. Reb had begun to pull on his dick as he watched, his desire erupting over his hand as they climaxed at the same time.

'Turn over,' Cody had ordered her, pushing Reb out of the way and putting a large hand on the flat of her back, forcing her to rest her palms on the bed. Talia had complied, juices coating the inside of her legs as she quivered in anticipation of his touch. But he'd taken his time, lining himself up carefully before pulling her head back by the hair he had bunched in his fist and ramming his cock into her as hard and fast as he could.

And, that time, she did scream.

* * * *

The following night, Reb turned up alone halfway through the evening. Talia looked over his shoulder expectantly.

'Cody's not coming,' he said. 'He had a bit of a fall. Horse banged him up pretty bad.'

'Oh God. Is he ok?' Talia was genuinely distressed at the thought.

'He's in the hospital. He broke his arm, but they are only keeping him in for the night due to the fact he was knocked unconscious.'

'What do you mean 'only'?'

Reb laughed. 'I thought you were gonna pass out, I just wanted to reassure you it wasn't anything serious.'

'Oh, poor Cody,' she said.

'Poor me, you mean. Man, that guy has been like a bear with a sore head since the accident. Anyone would think I pushed him off the damn horse.'

Talia felt a little guilty; she hadn't considered Reb's feelings at all. 'Are you ok?'

'A little shaken up. Thought he was a goner for a moment back there. The horse damn near fell on him.'

'Here, drink this,' she said, putting a shot of whisky in front of him.

'Thanks, I could use it.'

She poured one for herself, raising a toast to Cody's good health before knocking it to the back of her throat and swallowing on a grimace.

'You're an interesting woman,' Reb said appreciatively as she slammed her empty glass onto the counter. She smiled benignly, thoughts elsewhere.

'I'm so glad I didn't see him fall yesterday,' she said, thinking back to how scared she had been for him.

Reb laughed. 'Yeah, he told me you were watching him through your fingers.' He shook his head as he imagined it. 'You do realize you can still see what's happening when you do that right?' She punched him in the arm as he continued to tease her by peering at her through his own fingers from time to time; not stopping until he'd made her laugh.

'Do you think he would mind if I visited him?' she said, worry for Cody sobering her quickly.

'Who the hell knows, but I doubt it.' He laughed. 'I'll warn you though; he can be difficult when he wants to be.'

'Why is he so mad at you?'

Reb shrugged. 'Beats me. We were talking about how long it would take for his arm to get better. Then I mentioned you and that I was gonna come over tonight and let you know. That's when he got all bent out of shape.'

'Because you were coming over here?'

Reb nodded. 'I guess so.'

Talia fell silent. Was Cody jealous at the thought of her spending time alone with Reb? She rejected the idea.

'So, you got anything planned for tonight after you close up?' Reb asked.

Talia could see the hope in his eyes and, for the first time, she realized she wasn't remotely interested if Cody wasn't involved. 'Not tonight.' She smiled to soften her words. 'The last couple of days have taken it out of me. I could do with turning in early.'

'Ok. Sure.' He looked a little disappointed, but she didn't feel bad. Plenty of women had been eyeballing Reb from the minute he'd walked in. Guys who looked like he did only slept alone if they wanted to.

'Hey, Cindy,' she called, gesturing to the pretty blonde behind the bar that she should come join them. 'Have I introduced you to Reb yet?' she asked as the woman approached shyly.

Cindy shook her head, smiling up at the tall man in awe. 'Hi, Cindy,' he said, throwing a look at Talia that told her he knew what her game was, but he was gonna let her get away with it. 'Can I buy you a drink?'

Chapter 6

'What do you want?' Cody barked as Talia entered his hospital room early the next morning.

'I...I came to see how you were,' she said, wondering both at her own sanity and at what in the hell he was sore at her about. He looked pale and drawn. Maybe he felt as bad as he looked. That would explain his mood.

'Well, as you can see, I am fine.' His face set into a hard line as he fixed his eyes on the TV screen above the bed.

Talia fought back the urge to cry, determined not to show Cody that he'd upset her. 'Ok, well I didn't mean to annoy you. Reb told me last night that you'd had an accident—'

'So you guys still got together?' he interrupted harshly.

'I just told you, he came over.'

'Did he stay the night?'

For the first time since she'd walked in, his attitude made her angry. *Who did he think he was?* 'How is that any of your business? You don't own either of us.'

His usually warm brown eyes went hard and dark, making Talia glad he was confined to bed. 'You're right. It's nothing to do with me if you want to fuck each other's brains out.'

'Why do you care? You were the one who seduced me without telling me that you had a thing going with your buddy. One minute I was kissing you, the next you and Reb were talking me into spending the night with both of you.'

'You didn't take much convincing, lady.'

Talia's cheeks burned. How dare he treat her this way? 'That's because I thought I could trust you,' she said, tears making her voice tremble.

Some of the anger left Cody's face. 'Aw, shit, Talia. Don't cry.' He reached out a hand to grab hers, but she jumped away as if scalded. 'It's just that Reb—'

'Don't touch me,' she hissed, rubbing an angry fist across her face, wiping away tears she hadn't wanted to give him the satisfaction of seeing. 'In fact, don't ever come near me again.' She ran from the room, hearing his voice calling her back, but desperate to get away from the derision in his eyes.

Talia spent the rest of the day trying to figure out what his problem was. It was Cody's idea to seduce her, or at least it had seemed that way. Maybe Reb was the instigator and just left his buddy to do the ground work? Either way, he was the reason anything had happened at all and his attitude now beggared belief.

How many times had they done this kind of thing? From the way they had driven her crazy almost without words, they seemed very practiced at the art of sharing a woman. Talia got hot as she remembered Reb helping Cody when he put his head between her legs and the way they had swapped positions so that one could fuck her as she went down on the other.

But she also remembered the way Cody had said that he hadn't wanted to share. *What had he meant?* Maybe she got stuck in the middle of some macho game between them. Talia had no idea what his problem was, but she was damn sure it wasn't her.

The realization that it actually mattered to her what he thought didn't sit easy. They'd only known each other a few days but Talia knew that he was the only reason she'd been interested in their proposition that night. It was all about Cody for her. Just her luck that he didn't feel the same way if his earlier attitude was anything to go by.

Reb didn't help things by turning up again later that day. 'Did you go to see him?'

'Yes.' Her tone was curt. It wasn't Reb's fault that his friend was such an arrogant prick, but she just couldn't help directing some of her anger his way. Her head hurt from spending all evening thinking about the pair and she needed somewhere to vent her frustration.

He smiled, taking off his hat to run a hand through his hair, blowing out a long breath. 'Do I take that to mean it didn't go well?'

'What I don't get,' Talia said, ignoring his words, 'is why he's so damn mad at me. Last time he was here, he seemed happy enough. What happened?'

'What did he say to you?'

'He wanted to know if you had spent the night. When I told him it was none of his damn business, he got really mad.'

Reb looked around the bar, giving the few remaining patrons an irritated look. 'We need to talk, but it's too busy here. Can you come by my trailer after you get off work?'

'I won't finish till late, is that ok?' Talia didn't know what she expected to hear, but her interest was piqued. Reb left after giving her directions, kissing her cheek in a very chaste way considering what they'd already shared.

She locked the bar a couple of hours later and made her way through the quiet streets. Reb's trailer was easy enough to find and she knocked nervously on the door.

Voices approached from the other side and she realized he wasn't alone. Before the thought could form in her mind about who he was with, Cody opened the door.

Chapter 7

'Is he always that rude?' Talia asked after Cody had brushed passed her without saying a word, leaving her staring at an empty doorway.

'Not usually. I don't know what's got into him.' Reb took her hand, guiding her up the steps before closing the door and offering her a seat.

Talia could tell she was in male territory. Clothes were strewn over every surface, fighting for space with empty beer cans. A dog-eared calendar featuring naked girls hung from the wall of a kitchen containing a sink piled to the top with dirty dishes. Saddles, ropes, boots and gloves seemed to have pride of place on a fold down table, nestled between torn seating covered in mountains of papers, magazines and books.

Reb took a seat beside her after balling up some clothing and moving it out of the way. 'Sorry,' he said, looking around. 'We don't get visitors very often.'

'We?'

He nodded. 'Cody and I share this trailer.'

'You live like this all the time?'

'Only when we are on the road. Do you want something to drink?' he asked, gesturing toward a refrigerator. 'I'm pretty sure we only have beer.'

Talia shook her head quickly. 'No, I can't stay. What is it you wanted to talk about?'

'Why can't you stay?' Reb asked, crestfallen. Talia's stomach hit her boots. Had his intention in inviting her over tonight been to seduce her? She hoped not. She had no intention of allowing either of them to get that close again.

'I just can't,' she said, letting the silence hang between them as she hoped he would get to the point.

The smile returned, never absent for long. 'I think I know why Cody is so mad at us.'

'Mad at us? Why?'

'Just before he had his accident, we'd been talking about you.' Reb dropped his head, slight color flushing his cheeks. 'I told him I didn't want him seeing you anymore.'

'What?' Talia shook her head, showing him she didn't have a clue what he was getting at.

'I told him that I was, you know, interested in you and wanted to see where things could lead.'

'Oh God,' she said, running a hand through her hair. 'Look, Reb—'

'I know it sounds arrogant. I mean, I have no reason to believe you'd want me. I just needed him to back off and give me a free run.'

'Look, Reb, I'm not really interested in anything more serious.'

'Is it me?' His smile got shaky at the corners. Talia felt awful and rushed to reassure him.

'No, it's not you. I told you both; I don't need a man around to complicate things for me.' She gave his hand a squeeze to take the sting out of her words. 'I mean, look how this has turned out. Besides, you barely know me.'

He didn't return her laugh. 'Shit, Talia. I'm not asking for marriage, just a chance to see where this leads. Cody wasn't pleased when I asked him to back off, but at least he understands what I am feeling.'

'What did he say?' Talia didn't have time to question why she cared. All she knew was she was desperate to hear Cody's thoughts.

'At first, he tried to talk me out of it, said we weren't going to be around long enough for anything to happen. I told him I'd find a way to make it work—maybe come back to town in between runs. That's when his attitude changed and he said he didn't give a fuck what we did.' Reb looked as confused as she felt.

'Maybe he doesn't want things to change. He seems happy to live and work with you, as well as the other things you guys do together.' Talia felt her cheeks go red. How did she ever think she was sophisticated enough to handle a situation like this as casually as they seemed to? Despite what Cody had said, she was really a good girl at heart.

'It's not like it's the first time this kind of thing has come up,' Reb said, rejecting her words. 'I fall in love at the drop of a hat. Sorry, I wasn't talking us,' he said quickly, laughing when she rolled her eyes. 'All the other times, he didn't care either way.'

'How many times were there?'

'That I fell in love?'

'No, that you—you know—shared.'

Reb blushed again as if knowing she wouldn't like his answer. 'All the time.' He rushed to explain as he saw her shocked reaction. 'Hell, we've been hanging around the rodeo since we were kids and we both had our fair share of women. Even that can get boring when you do it too much. Then one night last year in Texas, a hot senorita took us both back to her place and blew our freaking minds. We been doing it ever since, but only when we meet someone we both want to —you know.'

'Fuck?' she asked, arching an eyebrow as he left the sentence hanging. 'And how often do these women agree to go along with it?'

'We haven't struck out yet.' He smiled before realizing it was the wrong thing to say. 'What I mean is –'

Never mind,' she said, getting to her feet. 'I was crazy to get anywhere near you two.'

Talia slammed her way out of the trailer, ignoring Reb's voice as she ran through the fields, back toward Main Street.

Chapter 8

Talia didn't plan to open the bar when she got up the next day, so she pulled on a jogging suit and flopped down in front of the TV, intent on enjoying a few hours of mindless soaps. She knew it was insane to lose the money that the extra trade increased by the Rodeo's last day would bring in, but she didn't care. Cody and Reb would be leaving town tomorrow—if not for good, then at least until the next County Fair—and her life could return to normal. But normal didn't seem so appealing now and, deep down, she knew why.

She was falling for Cody. Talia prided herself on her smarts, but this time they had let her down badly. Falling for a guy so jaded with life that he wasn't even looking for love anymore was crazy.

Falling for a guy who wasn't interested enough in her to want to make love to her alone. Even Reb, with all his boyish charm and happy demeanor, had tried to take things further than that when he mistakenly misread her reactions, assuming the chemistry was between her and him, not her and Cody.

At least she was consistent, she thought ruefully. Her ex hadn't wanted her either, but for an altogether different reason. Once she'd shut off the supply of money and free booze he thought her owning a bar entitled him too, he'd lost interest. Brett had never really loved her, Talia knew that now.

By late evening, the walls in her apartment had started to crowd in on her, so she wandered down into the bar, intent on doing some of the cleaning that was long overdue. The wooden counter was crying out to be treated with oil, and the floor behind it needed to be buffed.

She hoped the extra exertion would help her to sleep better than she had the last few nights.

She'd just dragged her cleaning kit out of the small cupboard at the end of the bar when a she heard a knock on the window and looked up to see Reb peering through it.

'That's all I need,' Talia said under her breath as she moved to open the door, jumping back as he almost fell into the bar, hand pressed against his face. 'What the hell happened to you?'

'Cody,' Reb said, walking passed. 'He slugged me.' His eye was starting to close and the bruising around it was red and angry.

'Have you had that looked at?' Talia guided him down onto a kitchen stool as she tilted his face up to the light.

'It only just happened.'

'Why the hell did he hit you?' she asked angrily. Violence appalled her.

'You,' he said, giving her a mock hurt look.

'Me?'

'Well, sorta. He saw me with Cindy after the show. Came right up to me, asked where you were and what in the hell I thought I was doing. I told him to get lost.' Reb smiled as he took the ice pack Talia gave him. 'Guess that wasn't such a good idea huh?'

'But why hit you?'

'Damned if I know. I've never seen him raise a hand to anyone before.'

Talia dabbed at the small cut on his brow with a wet cloth. 'This looks bad, Reb. You may need a couple of stitches.'

'Nah, I've had plenty of knocks over the years dealing with the horses. This will heal in a day or two.' He grimaced as she applied an alcohol swab, pressing down on the wound a little to make sure it was clean. 'Besides, it could have been worse. He could have hit me with his cast.'

Talia laughed, despite herself. 'You nut,' she said, mussing his hair before slapping him across the back of the head as a thought hit her. 'Hey, what were you doing with Cindy? Got over me damn quick, didn't you?'

He shrugged his shoulders. 'You made yourself pretty clear last night, Talia. I guess I didn't think you'd mind, especially as you were the one that introduced us.'

'Don't be silly. I'm pleased you and Cindy are getting on. Will you be seeing each other again?'

'Probably not,' he said, the humor leaving his face. Reb ran a finger down her arm, bringing her eyes back to his. She could see the invitation in his gaze, but she moved away, unwilling to give him the wrong idea. Reb sighed, but didn't push it further, staring at her for a moment longer before reaching for his hat and getting to his feet.

'I guess I better get going,' he said, moving towards the door. 'We're leaving town tomorrow, gotta get an early start.'

'Well take care of yourself,' Talia smiled, unsure what to say to someone she'd been so intimate with, but barely knew.

'Thanks for—you know,' he said, pointing to his eye.

'No problem.'

'Ok, I'll see you soon,' he said, kissing her cheek as they reached the doorway.

'Not that soon surely?' she said, wondering what he could mean.

'Oh didn't I tell you? Cody's staying in Chelwood for a while. Just as well seeing as he wants to knock my head off. The boss says the insurance won't cover him so he has to stay here till the doc says he's fit to travel. We are swinging back round to pick him up next week.'

'Oh,' Talia said, thoughts crashing through her head as she took in his words. Shutting the door on Reb moments later, she tried to suppress the butterflies in her stomach, certain there was no point in feeling excited at the news that a man who despised her was staying in town.

Chapter 9

'Why the hell didn't you tell me nothing happened?' Cody said as he stormed through the door as soon as she'd opened the bar the next afternoon.

Talia was taken aback, both by his presence and the tone of his voice. Why was he always so angry at her? 'You never gave me a chance.'

'Well, that's as may be but I sure wish you'd told me.'

'Why? What difference would it have made?'

Cody dropped his head, hiding his eyes under the brim of his hat. 'I wouldn't have hit him for one thing.'

Talia put her hands on her hips. 'That was an awful thing to do. Poor Reb didn't deserve it.'

'I know, I know,' he said, his voice dropping to a reasonable volume. 'But it wasn't entirely my fault.'

'And how do you figure that one out?'

He took off his hat, wiping the sweat from his brow with the back of his free hand before putting it back on. 'I thought he was running around on you.'

'That's crazy. There was nothing going on between us.'

'I know that now,' he ground out, embarrassment making him cranky. 'But the last thing I knew was he'd asked me to back off and give him a chance to show you how he felt.'

'Yeah, he told me,' she said.

'And then at the hospital, when you said you'd seen him alone the night before, I figured you felt the same way.' Cody's eyes searched hers, looking for clues as to how she was reacting to his words.

'Anyway, by the time he told me you were coming to his trailer Wednesday night, I was convinced you guys were an item.'

Talia could see the confession was hard for him. So, he'd hit his friend and he felt like a fool. What did he hope to achieve by telling her? 'Well, I hope you apologized for hitting him.'

'Oh, I have,' he said. 'He came to me this morning and made me listen to him. Reb is the reason I am here. I owe you both an apology.'

'Yes, you do,' she said, unwilling to let him off the hook so easily. 'I have a question though. Why do you care if he was fooling around?'

Cody smiled and the tension eased from his face as he took a step towards her. 'C'mon Talia, don't make me say it.'

'I think you better,'she said, beginning to smile herself. Talia moved away as he approached, backing up until the wooden counter stopped her progress. 'I want to be real clear that I understand what you are saying.'

His gaze dropped to her mouth as the space between them narrowed to mere inches. 'I hit him because he took you away from me, then it seemed like he didn't want you at all.'

'He took me away from you?' Talia tilted her head, not allowing him to kiss her until he'd finished explaining.

Cody nodded, flicking his tongue out to catch her top lip as he breathed his words into her face. 'I wanted you for myself.'

Her insides began to coil as his heat seeped into her. His groin brushed against her as he moved closer still, placing a free hand into the small of her back to press him against her. 'Then why involve Reb at all?'

'I let him talk me into it that first night. I should have held my ground, told him he wasn't welcome this time.' He stole a kiss, smiling as she gasped in surprise and held him at bay with hands pressed against his chest. 'Then, when he beat me to the jump and asked me to back off, I thought I'd missed my chance.'

'Why didn't you tell him how you felt?' Talia laughed, realizing what she'd said. 'Scratch that, why didn't you tell me?'

Cody's eyes got darker, and his voice dropped to barely a whisper. 'I saw the way you reacted that night. Jesus, Talia, you were on fire and for all I knew, you wanted more of the same.'

'I did want more, but not of Reb,' she whispered, breath coming fast as her body reacted to both the nearness of him and the memories brought on by his words. 'The only thing I really remember about that night was you, everything else was a blur.'

He kissed her then, crushing her body with his, using his good hand to hold her head steady as his tongue teased her lips apart.

Someone cleared their throat from the direction of the doorway. 'Err, excuse me Miss, are you open?' An elderly couple hovered nervously, seeming unsure they should be there at all.

Cody took a step back as Talia pushed him away with a laugh. 'Yes. Please, come on in.'

'I better go,' Cody said after she'd served the customers. 'I gotta see the doc.'

'Are you coming back later?' she asked, trying unsuccessfully to hide the promise in her question.

'For a smart woman, you ask some damn fool questions,' he said, laughing as he strode out into the street.

Chapter 10

As it turned out, he hadn't come back. Instead, Talia went out on a date.

A phone call later in the evening from Cody informed her of his change of plans. 'I'm staying at the Wenger. Can you get someone to cover for you and come join me for dinner?'

Talia simply shut the bar. The trade had died almost as soon as the Rodeo left town. Her regulars would just have to understand.

As she walked into the foyer of the small hotel an hour later, Talia waved to the desk clerk, smiling secretly as she realized the news she'd met the cowboy there would be all over town by daybreak. Chelwood was way too small to have any kind of private life, but she didn't mind. She loved the place.

Cody stood as she entered the restaurant. Dressed in a t-shirt and jeans, but without his hat, he looked like a younger version of the man she'd seen earlier that afternoon. His broad smile made her insides tingle, but that was nothing compared to the reaction of her body when he let his eyes do a long, slow tour of her dress.

'Talia...wow,' he said with difficulty, his voice catching in his throat. 'You look amazing.'

Thrilled that she'd worn the only dress in her closet, Talia smoothed out invisible creases in the strappy black Lycra shift cut to mid thigh. The night was a warm one so she'd kept her arms bare save for a silver bangle that matched the choker at her neck. 'Thanks, you look great, too.'

'Yeah, sure,' he said, as he stood behind her to push in her chair. 'That's the problem with living on the road; you can't bring a lot of stuff with you.' He brushed her long hair out of the way to drop a light kiss on her bare shoulder before taking his seat.

'Well, I think you look fine,' she smiled, touched by his nervousness. Talia felt a little edgy herself, but the thought of finally being alone with him outweighed any doubts she may have had.

Cody poured her a glass of the wine already open on the table. He didn't look to have touched much of his. 'I want to keep a clear head,' he told her when she asked why. Talia's hand shook a little as he watched her lips close around the rim of her glass, eyes narrowing as she swallowed nervously.

'Are you ready to order,' the waiter asked, appearing out of nowhere.

'Give us a moment,' Cody replied, never taking his eyes from hers. 'Are you hungry?' he asked her when the waiter left. Talia nodded, leaning forward. 'For food I mean?' he asked with a slow smile, looking at her parted lips. 'Me neither,' he said, as she shook her head.

She surprised him by standing up suddenly and grabbing her purse. 'Bring the wine with you,' she ordered, picking up their glasses and striding from the room. Cody threw some bills on the table, and rushed to catch up to her.

Talia helped him unlock the door to his room when his injured arm gave him trouble. 'Are you sure you're ok?' she asked, watching as he rolled his shoulder as if to ease the pain.

'Yeah, just don't expect any acrobatics,' he warned, taking the glasses from her hands and placing them on the dresser with the wine as he kicked the door shut with a foot. He wrapped his good arm around her waist, pulling her to him roughly.

'You'll have to let me do all the work this time,' she smiled after he'd kissed her. Talia brushed her lips against his neck as she helped ease his t-shirt over his head, careful to avoid knocking his arm. She threw the garment across the room, dropping to her knees before him to open the belt of his jeans. The denim bulged forward invitingly and she couldn't resist grazing her teeth over the hardness it contained.

Cody groaned as she slid the zipper down, moving his pants out of the way to let his cock spring free. 'Baby, I love your mouth,' he said, as her lips closed around him. Talia moaned in the back of her throat as she took him as deeply as she could, eyes fixed on his reactions. The muscles of his abdomen quivered each time she pulled him out almost to the tip and then allowed him to slide in again. 'I gotta sit down.' He laughed as he started to sway above her.

Talia helped him out of his jeans and boots before getting to her feet and reaching for the zipper of her dress. 'I can do that,' he said, turning her around. Cody ran his tongue down the skin he'd exposed as he opened the garment, smoothing the straps from her shoulders and allowing the fabric to pool at her hips before turning her around.

He eyed her breasts, running his thumb over her nipple and then sliding a flat palm down her abdomen, letting it disappear inside her bunched up dress. Talia watched him expectantly, smiling as his eyes narrowed and he sank his teeth into his lower lip when he discovered she wore no underwear. 'I thought I'd make things a little easier for you,' she explained innocently, delighted by his reaction. 'Oh!'

Cody's fingers had wasted no time, sliding knuckle deep into her pussy. 'That's what happens to bad girls,' he said, as her head fell back, forcing her to clutch at his shoulders to steady herself as he continued to plunge in and out of her.

'Bed,' was all she was able to say, as she used her body to push him toward it. Cody's fingers slipped out of her and she groaned at their loss. Waiting until he'd scooted into the middle of the huge divan, Talia kicked off her dress and crawled over to kneel beside him.

'What do you want me to do?' she asked, smiling as he ran a hand through her hair, twisting the dark tresses around his fingers.

He pushed her head down towards his cock. Talia took him into her mouth immediately, bracing her hands on his thighs as she felt him lift one of her legs over his body before dragging her groin up toward his face. The bristles on his chin grazed the tender skin of her inner thighs seconds before his tongue flicked over her clit. She groaned and spread her legs further, welcoming the feel of his hot mouth on her.

She sucked him in, over and over again, using her hands to help hold him steady as his hips bucked beneath her. Talia had to lift her head when his thumb pressed into her vagina without warning, making her cry out and wiggle against his tongue, still lapping at her bud.

'Cody...Cody, I'm gonna come. Oh, I'm gonna come. So hard, so fucking hard,' she gasped, digging her nails into his thighs when he threw his arm over her ass, pinning her against his mouth. He sucked her clitoris between his lips, moving his head rapidly from side to side.

Talia took as much as she could before scrabbling away, too sensitive to allow him to go on. She fell onto the bed in a breathless heap, legs splayed across his abdomen and torso. 'Jesus,' she said as she stared at the ceiling in shock, laughing a little at the sheer intensity of her orgasm.

'I thought you were gonna do all the work,' Cody said, trying to drag her back on top of him with one arm. 'Come over here and fuck me, will ya?'

'Sorry,' she laughed, straddling him. His eyes burned into hers and he bit his lip again as he watched her hold his cock upright, wriggling her hips as she placed him at the entrance to her pussy. Her eyes flared when the first, thick inch of him stretched her wide and she held her breath as she pushed down, sheathing him completely.

'God, you're so wet.' He groaned hoarsely, using his good hand to hold her still as he shuddered inside her. 'So tight and wet.'

Talia leaned forward, bracing her hands on his wide chest as she began to rock against him, moaning a little with each thrust. Cody reached up, bunched her hair in his hand and used it to drag her body down to his, kissing her as their faces met. He took over, holding her against him with a strong arm across her back as his hips left the bed to plunge his prick into her over and over again.

She slipped her own hand between them, pressing her fingers against her mound, increasing the friction caused by his abdomen. Her other hand burrowed into his hair, anchoring her body against his thrusting.

'Are you gonna come?' he growled into her ear as her muscles began to pulsate around him. 'I can feel the spasms deep in your cunt.'

Cody's words tipped her over the edge and she lifted her head to push down against him, impaling herself on his shaft. She began to whine, unable to make any other sound as the breath left her lungs.

'Fuck,' he shouted as he exploded violently, digging his fingers into the skin of her ass to hold her close as he jerked into her. 'Fuck,' he said again as his body slumped back down to the bed, the last of his orgasm making him tremble beneath her.

Cody winced as his penis slipped out of her and Talia jumped away in alarm, mistaking the reason for his pain. 'Did I hurt your arm?'

He laughed, pulling her back against him to drop a kiss on her forehead. 'I was buried so deeply inside you, it took my breath away when I pulled out, that's all.'

Talia didn't need to be reminded - her own muscles were still adjusting to his withdrawal, taking a moment to get used to the loss. 'Is *that* what I could feel poking me in the back of my throat?' she giggled, jumping as he pinched her butt in reply.

By the time the dawn came, they finally managed to fall asleep after making love to the point of exhaustion.

And Talia was right—she and the cowboy were the talk of the town.

Chapter 11

By the time Reb rolled back into town a week later, Cody was living in Talia's apartment. They'd both agreed it was silly to spend the time apart, especially as he'd be hitting the road again soon.

'How are you gonna make this work?' Reb asked, when Cody told him, in front of Talia, that they intended to keep seeing each other.

'We've only got two more months till the end of this run, and then I'm hanging up my spurs.'

'You're quitting the Rodeo?' Talia asked, as surprised as Reb by the news. 'When did you decide this?'

'Couple days ago,' he smiled, looking from one to the other.

'What are you gonna do?' Reb demanded, annoyance masking his handsome face. 'This is all we know.'

'Yeah, which is exactly the reason why it's time to move on,' Cody said, putting a hand on his friends shoulder. 'Don't know about you buddy, but I think it's time I put down some roots.'

Reb smiled, throwing his arm around Cody. 'I guess you know what you want,' he said, casting a warm look at Talia, 'but it won't be the same without you.'

'I'll miss you, too, Reb. We've been together a long time.'

Talia started humming the theme to 'Love Story', jumping out of the way with a laugh as Cody threw a bar towel at her. 'See what I gotta put up with?' he asked Reb with a smile.

'You look like you can handle it,' he replied, giving Talia a wink, holding her gaze just a moment longer before turning back to this friend. 'So, are you ready to hit the road one last time?'

'Just gotta get my stuff and say my goodbyes.'

Reb took the hint, bidding Talia farewell and telling Cody he'd wait in the truck.

'Don't be too hard on him,' she said as she watched Reb walk away. 'I don't think he ever meant to come between us.'

'I'd trust him with my life,' Cody assured her, pulling her into the gap between his legs as he leaned against the bar. 'I backed off because he asked me to and I know he'll do the same for me.'

Talia wrapped her arms around his neck, forcing his dark head down to hers to kiss him. Cody picked her up from the floor, bringing their faces level, groaning as a horn sounded in the street reminding them both that he had to leave.

'Are you really coming back?' she asked five minutes later, as he walked toward the door, needing to hear him say the words despite his earlier conversation with Reb.

He laughed, pulling his hat down over his eyes. 'What is it with you and stupid questions?'

THE END

Siren Publishing

Ménage Amour

Luxie Ryder

Two Cowboys

for Christie

TWO COWBOYS FOR CHRISTIE

Midnight Cowboys 2
LUXIE RYDER
Copyright © 2009

Prologue

One night in a barn many years ago…

Christie took a big swallow from the jug Garrett had handed to her. She tried her best to force the potent liquid down her throat but couldn't stop a gasp escaping from her lips as it burned its way to her gut. 'Great,' she said in as strong a voice as she could manage, desperate not to let Garret and Connor think she wasn't up to the challenge.

To her annoyance, they laughed at her anyway. 'Well, I didn't see you drink any,' she challenged Connor, thrusting the jug of moonshine towards him.

'Surprised there's any left after the birthday boy here poured most of it down his throat,' Connor said then smirked as he noticed the condition of his cousin. Garrett had a sloppy grin on his face and his blue eyes were glazing over. 'We should share the rest. I think he's had enough.'

Garrett protested. 'Hey, I'm the only one old enough to be drinking.'

'Only by a day,' Christie reminded him, 'and anyway, I bet you had a drink when you were my age.'

'At 19, I knew I was still a kid,' he teased, flinching as she punched him in the arm.

'You may be the oldest but that doesn't mean you know best,' she said with a smile, using a phrase she must have said to him a hundred times over since they'd first met as kids.

The three of them had snuck away from the birthday party and into the barn after Connor had stolen the moonshine. Christie thought the boys looked very in handsome in their new shirts, jeans and boots. They'd even bought new hats and cut their shaggy blonde hair. Seeing them so looking so smart was a welcome change from the scruffy work clothes they usually wore. Secretly, she thought they looked pretty great in those too.

She knew she looked nice in her party dress. Many of the older party goers had told her the pale green watered satin looked pretty against her red hair. It was the first 'grown up' dress she had ever owned and she felt very adult and glamorous wearing it.

'I'll be 21 before the end of the year,' Connor said to nobody in particular, ignoring Garrett's outstretched hand and passing the moonshine back to Christie. She laughed as she shook the jug, realizing it was almost empty and that he'd taken almost as much as Garrett.

'This must be my share,' she said, tipping her head back and allowing the alcohol to pour down her throat.

'Christie, be careful,' Garrett warned, edging towards her.

Connor made a grab for the jug. 'Seriously Christie, stop it.'

She continued to drink, fighting the burning sensation it was causing and wriggling out of their grasps as each of them tried to take the moonshine away. Finally, Garrett lurched forward, dragging her hand away from her mouth as Connor pinned her to the hay.

'She drank it all,' Garrett said to Connor, turning the jug upside down to show there wasn't a drop left. Christie giggled.

'You see that Garrett? She thinks she's funny,' Connor said, laughing as he began to tickle her ribs. The other young man joined in the game, pinning her arms over her head to give Connor better access.

'Stop it,' she gasped through her laughter, 'you'll ruin my dress.' Thankful that they seemed to have stopped, she made to sit up before she realized Garrett had not yet let go of her hands. His gaze had dropped down to her neckline and he had become very still.

'That sure is a pretty dress,' he said quietly, bringing his eyes back up to hers.

'You do look beautiful,' Connor agreed, dropping down onto the hay and turning to lie next to her. Garrett released her hands and took the position on her other side.

Christie knew she was free to sit up but now, she didn't want to move. Suddenly, she was the focus of their undivided attention – attention she had craved for the last few years. The crush she'd had on them since the age of 15 had been near painful at times, especially as she'd been forced to endure watching them flirt with the local girls. She'd grown tired of being ignored by them because she was their tomboy sidekick and had begun to make subtle efforts to get their attention by doing her hair and dressing a little more feminine. Nothing had worked. But now, they were laying either side of her, telling her how pretty she was and looking at her in the way men should look at women. Christie loved every moment of it.

Garrett moved, trapping one of her long red curls in his fingers. Christie turned towards him and had the breath knocked from her lungs as she saw the expression in his eyes. She hadn't had much experience but she sure knew what that look meant – he wanted to kiss her. She closed the distance between them when she saw a resolve settle across his features and knew he wasn't going to act on the urge. Christie kissed him quickly, before her nerve could desert her and it gratified her to hear his sharp intake of breath. Her closed lips pressed against his for a moment until she felt him pull away.

She kept her eyes closed, frightened she would find him laughing at her but instead he spoke.

'If you're gonna kiss me, do it properly.'

Christie felt his hand grasp her jaw and she opened her eyes just in time to see him tilt his face towards hers. Their lips touched again, but this time, he was kissing her. His mouth moved softly over hers, gently prizing her lips apart and she gasped as she felt the tip of his tongue touch hers. His strong hand slid down the column of her neck and over her arm, his thumb just brushing across the rise of her breast as it passed. Christie squirmed against the heat building between her legs and swallowed a groan as she felt his palm slide over her butt and he pulled her closer to him.

Suddenly, a new sensation joined the ones already overwhelming her. Connor's lips grazed across her neck just before his body slid behind hers. She felt his erection pressing into her butt and wondered if Garrett knew what was happening. She opened her eyes again to see Garrett's gaze flash in Connor's direction, but it didn't seem to bother him and he still continued to kiss her. If anything, he became more intense, pressing himself harder against her.

Christie felt safe, protected and worshipped and the thought that she shouldn't really be doing this with both of them was chased away by the sensations they were causing in her. Connor pulled at her leg, dragging it back across his thighs and allowing his hand access to her groin, still covered by clothing. He brushed his fingers over her mound through the fabric and Christie reacted so strongly that she had to tear her mouth away from Garrett's and moan out loud.

Her torso was exposed, allowing Garrett more access and he'd just placed a tentative hand over her breast when suddenly, he froze and began to push her away. He fell onto his back in the hay with a hand thrown across his face as if refusing to look at her.

'What's wrong?' she asked, terrified that she had either done something badly or that her inexperience was showing. Connor stopped his actions and looked over her shoulder at his cousin, his ragged breath blowing hard in her ear.

'Get away from her,' Garrett said without looking at them. Christie felt a moment of resistance from Connor but he eventually pulled away with an angry grunt.

She sat up slowly as Connor got to his feet and walked over to his cousin, kicking the sole of his boot hard to get his attention. 'I'm getting pretty damn tired of you telling me what to do Garrett,' he warned, the anger in his voice making it tremble.

Garrett jumped to his feet and squared up to Connor and Christie was sure he would hit him. She found her legs and got in between them. 'Stop it!' she shouted.

'Straighten your dress,' Garrett said, flicking his eyes away as if the sight of her disgusted him.

'Don't tell her what to do,' Connor said. She was smart enough to know he wasn't really defending her. He was just adding more fuel to the fire to infuriate his cousin. 'Who the hell do you think you are?'

Garrett took a threatening step towards him and Christie tried again to get between them. A firm push on her shoulder sent her stumbling across the barn but she kept her feet. 'Go home,' Connor bellowed at her.

Tears threatened but she wouldn't cry in front of him. She hated him - hated both of them in fact. Christie did up the stray buttons on the front of her dress and smoothed down her hair before walking from the barn with as much dignity as she could muster. She let the door swing wide as she pushed through it, waiting until she heard it slam shut behind her before allowing the tears to come.

She ran home that night, sure she would never hurt as much again as she did right at that moment. The boys she adored – the ones she loved more than herself – had just rejected her and life would never be the same again.

Chapter 1

Fifteen years later…

Christine Shepherd took a big gasp as she tried to stop her head spinning. She'd just been charged and then bear-hugged by two boys who'd grown into big handsome men since she'd last seen them and the experience had nearly taken her breath away.

'Whoa! Guys, put me down,' she pleaded as the pair took turns in lifting her from the floor in over enthusiastic greeting. 'Garrett! Stop that!'

The taller, older of the two did as he was told although never quite letting her go. 'Damn, Christie. It's good to see you.' His handsome face split into an ear to ear grin and he barely looked a day older than he had fifteen years earlier.

'Sure is,' agreed Connor, almost as reluctant to let go when he got his turn to hug her. 'How long has it been?'

'Too long,' she smiled, reclaiming her arms and folding them quickly in case they were tempted to trap her between them again.

'The years have been good to you.' He smiled, giving a long low whistle as he looked her over. 'You still look sixteen.'

'Liar,' Christie said, punching him playfully in the arm. The temptation to muss his wavy blond hair fled as her fist made contact with a wall of solid muscle. Wow. Since when had Connor been so built? Cornflower blue eyes locked on hers as he noticed her reaction.

'Guess I filled out, huh?' As much a boast as a statement, it seemed Connor was mighty proud of his body, and so he should be Christie thought as she took the time to look at him properly. 'Filled out' wasn't nearly enough of a phrase to describe what had happened to the scrawny kid she'd played with all those years ago.

'He's not bad for a little 'un,' she heard Garrett say, dragging her attention back to him. Christie looked at him with new eyes too. Damn! What did they put in the water around these parts? Even bigger and stronger than Connor, Garrett's hair was a shade darker than his cousin's wheat blond but he had the same piercing blue eyes that they had both inherited from their grandfather. They looked more like brothers than cousins.

Thinking about their Wyler heritage reminded her of the reason she'd come home after all this time. 'How is she?'

'Mom's coping ok,' Garrett said, kicking at the dust with his boot. Christie could see that he still wouldn't allow those close to him to know when he was hurting. 'Pa's death is a blessed relief for both of them. He couldn't handle anymore pain and she sure couldn't handle watching him suffer.'

'Poor Maisie.' Christie had never been close to the woman but her heart went out to her. Nobody deserved to watch their big, strong, larger-than-life husband waste away, ravaged by the cruel cancer that had spread through him. Now in her late sixties, Maisie must have found nursing him absolutely exhausting, both mentally and physically.

'It means a lot to Garrett that you came back for the funeral,' Connor said as if sensing his cousin found it hard to say the right words. 'It means a lot to all of us.'

'I loved Winston like an uncle. I had to be here.'

Christie waited for Garrett to look at her again, but he'd hidden his eyes under the brim of his hat. She could see a muscle flexing in his strong, wide jaw and the grim set of his lips. Searching out Connor's eyes, she found him gesturing that they should just head for the house.

'You sure are a sight for sore eyes,' Connor said again. He stood to one side to allow her access to the front steps leading up to the big, rambling ranch house. 'Although I don't remember you being a brunette.' His gaze was teasing as he allowed it to drift over her long, sleek hair.

'The red is still there.' She laughed. 'It's just really well hidden.' Garrett chuckled behind them, making it clear his moment of sadness was over.

'You're too skinny,' he said, running his eyes over her 5'9' frame. Christie couldn't argue with him. The trauma she'd gone through the last couple of years had cost her twenty pounds she hadn't needed to lose. Still, it wasn't polite to point it out and she told him so with a laugh.

'We've put you in your old room,' he said, smiling apologetically as he changed the subject. She'd known where she'd be staying as soon as she agreed to come. Many a time during the years they'd grown and played together, she'd spent the night in their parents' house. The Wyler ranch had bordered her father's until the day her family had been forced to move away due to the bank calling in the loan. By that time, she had married and moved to another town.

Connor's parents had died when he'd been barely more than a baby and Maisie and Winston had taken him in, raising him like a younger brother to Garrett. There was only 8 months age difference between them but neither really looked as if they were just a couple of years off forty.

'Where's your mom?' Christie asked, surprised to find the kitchen that formed the heart of the big rambling house empty.

'She's staying with her sister in town,' Connor said. 'She just couldn't face being here alone while we were out working the ranch.'

'I think she should live with Aunt Claire from now on,' Garrett added. 'There's nothing for her to do out here now Pa's gone.'

'Have you suggested that?' she asked gently, aware that the Wyler men didn't always speak their minds.

'Not yet.' Connor smiled. 'We were kinda hoping that Aunt Claire would do it for us. You know Ma; she's as stubborn as a mule.'

'Yeah, but can you blame her?' Christie smiled as she reminded them both what nightmares they had been as kids. 'Look what she had to put up with.'

'Hey, we weren't that bad,' Garrett protested, swatting her behind with his hat.

Later, alone in the pretty room that still had the flowered wallpaper, drapes and bedcovers she remembered from her childhood, she realized just how much she had missed Catron County and the two men.

Remembering how crazy in love she had once been with both of them made her heart beat a little faster and brought a smile to her face. Christie felt a ripple of heat go through her as she remembered how big and strong they were now. The pair had always been handsome boys but they'd grown into very attractive men. Years of hard work out in the New Mexico sun had made them bronzed and hard. Christie was glad her raging, teenage hormones hadn't been subjected to such an overdose of testosterone. If she met either of them now as strangers, she doubted her thirty-six year old hormones would fare much better.

The memory of a night she had never been able to forget came crashing back, spurred on by the thoughts of how sexy they'd become. Things had gotten out of hand after a birthday party and she'd found herself alone in the barn with Garrett and Connor. The boys had stolen some moonshine and they'd all been a little tipsy. All Christie actually remembered were a few fumbles and kisses but she'd learned an important lesson. If Garrett and Connor had tried to take it any further, she would have been powerless to resist. She was glad now that they'd stopped short of actually doing anything, but to this day, she knew things wouldn't have ended where they did if left to her. With nothing more intense than a few chaste kisses, they had turned her on to the point of abandon.

Christie had been unable to think of them in the same way after that, and no longer as older 'brothers' who watched out for her. To her teenage eyes, they'd turned into men and feelings that she didn't understand flip-flopped in her stomach whenever they got near.

She gazed out of the window, enthralled once more by the view she had never quite forgotten. The irregular shaped valley that the Wyler Ranch had shared with her father was surrounded by mountains and high ridges. The northern end of the spread opened out into meadow with Ponderosa pines, aspens, oaks and firs lining the hillsides. The two-track road she'd just arrived on wound its way lazily through the center of the valley before finally disappearing behind a mountain.

When her husband had moved them both out to Albuquerque, over 200 miles away, she'd always known she would be back one day but not for such a sad reason. The dream of raising the money to buy back her father's ranch had long since faded as property prices soared and the income from farming continued to fall. By then she had divorced the man she knew by that time to be the lowest example of a human being she'd ever had the misfortune to come across, and her priorities had changed. Getting away from Jack in one piece had consumed her thoughts for the last couple of years.

Christie smiled as she imagined what two magnificent male specimens like Connor and Garrett would make of the slightly effeminate, metrosexual Jack. What she'd once thought was suave sophistication turned out to be just plain old fashioned vanity. And the 'pretty' man had an ugly soul. She hoped his recent silence meant he'd given up stalking her with his attempts at reconciliation. She blew away the thoughts of him, determined to use her time in the wilds of New Mexico to get him out of her system once and for all and find herself again.

Chapter 2

Supper was interesting. Christie didn't know what she'd expected when she heard they were having chili but it sure didn't look anything like the brownish red sludge on her plate. She stared at it for a moment, unsure if her desire to please Connor by eating the meal he'd prepared outweighed her fear of actually putting any of it in her mouth.

'We never learned to cook,' Garrett said when he saw her reaction. 'Ma's always done it.'

'It doesn't taste as bad as it looks,' Connor offered, scooping a large spoonful into his mouth.

'I sure hope not,' Christie said under her breath. She felt a kick under the table and looked up to find Garrett shaking his head almost imperceptibly as if warning her to shut up.

'We don't usually bother much if Ma isn't here but Connor wanted to welcome you properly.'

Christie realized that Connor was trying to please her, hence Garrett's warning. 'Well, it's very kind of you.' She smiled, forcing herself to eat. Connor had been right. It didn't taste too bad at all and Christie found herself hungry enough to clear her plate, pleasing him in the process.

'You know, he used to have the biggest crush on you,' Garrett said as Connor left the room for a moment after they'd cleared the table.

'Me?' she said dumbly, unsure why he'd chosen to tell her that now.

He nodded. 'We both did.'

She didn't know what to say, so she said nothing. Garrett's eyes told her there was more to the story but he didn't share his thoughts. Christie wondered if he knew just how ironic their conversation seemed. One of the many reasons she'd stopped herself from staying in touch was the fact that, when she left and for a long time after, she'd been in love with them both.

In the years before she married and moved away, Christie had watched, sick with envy, as they began to show more interest in the girls in town. Large breasts and pretty hair suddenly impressed them more than a tomboy who could climb a tree or kill a rattlesnake as well as they could. Neither of them had seemed remotely interested in her anymore after that night in the barn and she blamed herself. Their lives had taken separate paths from that moment on and she hardly saw them anymore. A chasm had opened between her and the boys and they'd barely been on speaking terms when she'd first met Jack on a rare night out in town.

As a young kid, there had always been a part of her that believed she would be married to one of them when she grew up. Garrett had been her first choice back then but, even in her childish fantasies, she'd always known that Connor had a soft spot for her. The idea of being with him instead had made her almost as happy. But that was a lifetime ago. Now, it felt a little surreal to be sitting in their kitchen as a grown woman, remembering her young dreams and hearing about their old feelings for her.

'I can't believe you two are still single,' she said. The need to stop Garrett reading her thoughts as he stared deeply into her eyes had helped her to find her voice. 'Last time I looked, you two were all over the girls in town.'

'Connor almost bit the bullet once.' Garrett laughed, turning to explain the conversation to the other man as he walked back into the room. 'That's before he caught her in the back seat of Billy Ray's pick-up.'

Connor groaned. 'Don't remind me. I almost made the worst mistake of my life.'

Five minutes later, after they had moved out on to the porch to watch the setting sun, she found Garret watching her closely. 'What about you?' he asked. 'We heard things didn't work out with you and that guy—what was his name?'

'Jack.' Christie knew well and good that Garrett hadn't forgotten his name.

'Yeah, that's it. What happened?'

'That's one soap opera you don't need to hear about right now,' she said.

'You had problems?' Connor asked.

'Not so much these days. Jack is beginning to realize that it's over between us but he still turns up every now and then.'

'You divorced him?' Christie nodded in reply, unsettled by the interest in Garrett's gaze as he'd asked the question. 'Are you dating again?'

'No. Jack would have caused all kinds of problems if I'd tried to see anyone else. It just seemed easier to get him out of my life totally before I even thought about dating again. This last couple of weeks, I haven't seen him at all so maybe he has given up.'

'Sounds like a real piece of work, Christie. What in hell did you see in a guy like that?' Connor sounded angry.

'He wasn't like that in the beginning. He loved me, made me feel special, you know?' She looked from one to the other, wondering if they realized just how much of the way things had turned out was their doing. 'Isn't that what we all want?'

'You've always been special to us,' Garrett said.

She felt a blush creep over her cheeks. 'Thank you. You have always looked out for me and I appreciate it.'

'It's more than that, Christie.' Connor left the sentence hanging, allowing his words to sink in. Why were they talking this way?

Maybe grief was making them nostalgic for the past. 'We loved you too.'

'Still do.' Garrett said.

'Aw, thanks guys,' she said, unsure if she'd understood but choosing to play it down. 'I love you too.'

'We don't mean the kind of love you have for a kid sister, Christie. We are in love,' Garrett clarified.

She took another shaky breath as they watched for her reaction, pretty sure the confusion and surprise was written all over her face. 'Why are you telling me this now?'

'Because you're here. If you'd have come home sooner, we'd have told you then.' Connor looked to Garrett for agreement. 'We made ourselves a promise that if we ever saw you again we would tell you how we felt.'

'But it's been almost fifteen years.'

Garrett laughed. 'Don't I know it.'

Christie felt her temper begin to rise. 'Why in hell didn't you tell me this back then? Do you know how embarrassed I was, how humiliated I felt when you rejected me?'

Connor's brow knit into a confused frown. 'Rejected you? What in hell are you talking about?'

'That night in the barn.' Her cheeks flamed as she was forced to remember what had happened. She dropped her gaze. 'I'm not sure if you remember it as well as I do.'

'Jesus, Christie,' Garrett near shouted, 'of course we remember. That was the cause of all the problems.'

She squirmed in her seat, unsure if she could take a verbal rehashing of what had been one of the most painful experiences of her life.

'Nobody rejected you. Garrett stopped because he heard Pa calling. I didn't even know until he told me later. I guess you didn't hear him either?'

Garrett shook his head, as if he still couldn't believe what she'd said. 'That night, Connor and me had a huge fight over you.'

'Fight over me?' Christie said. She realized she sounded like a broken record but found it hard to do much more than repeat everything they said.

'You wore that pretty green dress and curled your hair. Then you danced with both of us,' Connor said, his eyes aglow with the memory. 'You'd just turned nineteen, Christie, and it was the first time either of us had noticed how much you'd grown up.'

She hoped they'd be kind enough not to mention what had happened next in detail. Both of the boys had been very attentive, even before they'd gone into the barn, hovering close by all evening. Back then, she'd put it down to nothing more than camaraderie, certain they had no idea of the huge crush she had on them both. When things had gotten out of hand, she'd blamed it on the drink.

Connor continued the story. 'Anyway, I made the mistake of telling Garrett after the party that I would marry you one day. His reply was 'like hell you will'.' The pair of them laughed, as if reminiscing about nothing more than an old hunting trip. 'So, we had a fight over you, right there in front of the house.' Connor used his bottle to point out across the yard.

'Pa came and separated us, whooped our behinds and told us no woman was worth losing family over.' Garrett said the words quietly but Christie heard the anger simmering beneath them. 'He'd figured out some of what we'd been up to in the barn and he tore a strip off us, saying we'd taken advantage of you. He was right. We were older and should have known better. He told us any fool could see that you had feelings for us and that the manly thing to do would be to stay away from you and give you time to grow out of it. Like fools, we agreed.'

Connor took up the story. 'By the time Pa finished, he'd made it sound like we had lured you into a trap and plied you with booze.

Every time I saw you after that, even though I wanted you badly, I just felt so guilty.'

'We both did.'

Christie was stunned. So they hadn't rejected her at all? Connor was right, she hadn't heard Old Man Wyler calling for them but it did explain why Garrett stopped what he was doing so suddenly.

'Is that why you are telling me this now, because your Pa has died?' Christie didn't believe either of the men had been afraid enough of their father to let him dictate who they could love or how to live their lives.

Connor shook his head. 'No, we decided way before then. The night before you got married, Garrett and me got stinking drunk and started to talk about you again for the first time in forever. We were sick with jealousy that you were marrying that jerk and we realized that neither of us had gotten over you.'

'It took a couple more years until we decided that we had to do something about it, Garrett said. 'Neither of us had moved on. So we agreed that, if things didn't work out for you and Jack, we were gonna come find you, tell you how we felt.'

'So why didn't you?'

'Because time passes and feelings get pushed to one side once work and family responsibilities take over. For the last few years, we've done nothing but run the ranch and support Ma in caring for our father. There wasn't much time for anything else. Besides, from what we heard in your mother's letters to our parents, you seemed happy with your husband.'

'But, now you are here.' Connor's face lit up with hope.

Christie fell silent, staring from one to the other in turn. What she'd just heard seemed insane. 'What do you want from me?' she said, still unsure what they were asking.

'We want to know how you feel.' Garrett leaned forward, pinning her to the chair with the intensity in his eyes. 'And we want to ask you to stay here with us. Don't go back to Albuquerque.'

'Stay? How the hell could I stay here now?' Christie began to shout as the old hurt and frustration returned. They had turned their backs on her when she needed them most. Ok, they had a damned good reason but she hadn't known that at the time. 'I had feelings— once—but you forced me to push them away. You wanted other girls, not me, and I learned to live with that. You can't just click your fingers and have me come running back here as if nothing had happened.'

'That's not what we are asking for, Christie,' Connor said patiently. 'Garrett is jumping the gun.' The look he gave his cousin spoke volumes, warning him to back off. 'First, we just need to know how you feel.'

'I feel cornered and confused,' she said, tiredness making her voice weak. Christie knew she had to be honest but speaking about the emotions she'd learned to bury deep inside her was hard after so long. 'As a kid, I used to hero worship you both and followed you around like a lovesick puppy. Then, as I started to get older, my feelings changed. You'd become men and I reacted to that. I began to have feelings—'

'So you felt the same?' Garrett interrupted.

'Yes, I did,' she agreed. 'But that was then, this is now.'

'What's changed? We're still the same people we always were,' Connor said.

'What's changed is that we're all grown up now and things are different. You turned your backs on me after that night. So I moved on.'

'I know and I am sorry,' Garrett said. 'If it's any consolation, we have suffered for our decision.'

'We've all suffered for it.' Christie couldn't keep the bitterness out of her voice.

'Then give us a chance to make it up to you,' Connor pleaded.

'This is crazy. I could never knowingly come between you even if I wanted to.'

'Why would you come between us?' Connor asked.

'Because I would be forced to choose, and I could never do that.'

Garrett sat back in his chair, face pensive as he ran his hands over his denim clad thighs nervously. 'Who's asking you to choose?'

Chapter 3

Who's asking you to choose?

The words ran through Christie's head over and over again throughout the long, almost sleepless night that had followed their conversation. Were they really suggesting she date both of them at the same time?

Even as her brain told her that she could never agree to such a thing, she caught herself thinking about what it would actually take to keep two men happy. Christie laughed aloud at one point as she imagined drawing up a schedule, giving each guy an alternate night but keeping Sunday for herself. Hey, a girl would need time to recover.

Had they already discussed who would spend the first night with her? Christie knew if left to her, she'd have a hell of a time deciding which one she wanted the most. Connor was the kind of guy you would turn to if you needed a confidence boost. His easy charm made a girl feel good. But Garrett—he could burn you up. He wasn't great with words but he made up for that in his actions. Whoever he dealt with knew exactly what he wanted from them. Christie didn't see any reason to doubt he'd be the same in bed.

By morning, she'd convinced herself that the grief of their recent loss had made them both a little reckless. Christie knew from the experiences of other friends and family that bereavement often gave people a desperate need to do something 'life affirming'.

She had very little time to think about what had happened for the rest of the day. The funeral had been scheduled for early morning. Connor and Garrett were due to leave just after she came down to breakfast and acted as if nothing untoward had happened. Neither of them mentioned the conversation they'd shared. This day was about something far more important and any unfinished business would have to wait.

'I'm not looking forward to this,' Garrett said, looking handsome and somber in his grey suit. Christie slid her arms up around his neck, finding it hard to reach but managing to force him down to her height for a hug. His initial resistance melted and she heard him sigh heavily as the tension eased out of him. Connor didn't resist her comforting touch. Unlike Garrett, he had no trouble in asking for what he needed. He squeezed her hard, only letting go when reminded it was time to head out.

She swallowed down the huge lump that formed in her throat as she watched them leave. Being the strong one was a new feeling for her. She'd always turned to Garrett and Connor for support in the past but she was glad to be there for them when they needed her.

Christie made her own way to the funeral. The boys had to travel with the procession and would meet up with her after the ceremony. She sat in the back pew of the church, tears welling in her eyes when she saw the pain etched on their faces as they passed by with the coffin held aloft.

The ceremony was a testament to the life Winston had led and many of his friends gave very moving speeches about him, but the family didn't speak. Christie imagined their grief ran deep and thought of her own parents, too busy to travel down to attend, and how she would feel in the Wylers' place.

By the graveside a short while later, she had a moment to focus on Connor and Garrett more closely. They seemed to be coping well, both of them determined to support their frail mother. She didn't look anywhere near as formidable as Christie remembered. Crumpled between her two sons, Maisie looked frightened and alone despite their comforting embraces.

'Hello dear, how lovely to see you. Thank you so much for coming,' she said to Christie as the mourners began to give their respects after the service. Her voice had taken on an automatic drone and Christie suspected she was barely managing to go through the motions of speaking to everyone.

'I'm fine, Mrs. Wyler. My parents couldn't make it but wanted me to send their love.'

Christie saw the recognition in her eyes and realized that Maisie hadn't even realized who she'd been speaking to so far. 'It's great to see you again, Christie,' she said with a weak smile. Christie squeezed her hand before moving along to allow others to pay their respects, turning to look for Maisie's sons. She found them standing at the graveside, Garrett's arm thrown around Connor in support. Christie didn't approach them as they said a private goodbye to their father.

They searched her out later, at the reception that had been organized in a local bar, after taking care of the guests and seeing their mother off to her sister's house. 'Sorry we've been ignoring you all day,' Garrett said.

'I understand.' Christie had kept her distance, partly because of the sad duties they had to fulfill but also because she felt in no rush to deal with the unspoken issue hanging between them. As the hours had passed, she had often turned to find either Garrett or Connor staring at her questioningly. She knew the conversation of the previous night was as much on their minds as it was hers. 'You look a lot less burdened now it's over,' she said, noting the color had returned to Garrett's cheeks and the old, familiar fire was back in his eyes.

He laughed. 'A lot of that has to do with the amount of liquor I've had.'

'Yeah, what is it with funerals?' Connor said as he joined them. 'Everybody keeps refilling your glass.'

Christie smiled, glad to see the guys were doing ok. 'So, I guess you are gonna need a ride home?'

'I'm gonna need a little more than that,' Garrett said darkly, making Christie's eyes clash with his. His lips had parted and she could feel his warm breath fanning her face as his gaze slid slowly down over her body.

As inappropriate as the timing of his comment was, Christie still felt her nipples pebble instantly and a flush bloom on her cheeks. 'You're drunk,' she whispered angrily, shame making her voice harsh.

'Not too drunk to know what I want,' he answered quietly, making sure with his gaze that she knew he'd noticed the reaction of her body. 'What's your excuse?'

'This isn't the time,' Connor warned him gently. Still, he moved to stand on Christie's other side, almost sandwiching her between him and his cousin. 'We'll talk later.' His eyes said more and she began to wonder just how much they had discussed between them.

A little later as they headed back to the ranch, Christie's anger was forgotten when she had to smile at the sight of the very tall Garrett squashed into the back seat of her compact car. 'You ok back there, big guy?'

'Don't push it,' he warned, his rueful grin the only thing visible under his Stetson. Garrett had decided to lie across the back seat after opening the window to put his booted feet through it and his hat had slipped down to cover most of his face.

Connor wasn't faring much better. His hat lay in his lap and, even with the front seat pushed back as far as he could get it his knees were almost up under his chin. 'I knew we shoulda taken the truck.'

'You'd both had too much to drink,' she reminded them.

'Not as much as you think. Garrett said he could drive but you wouldn't listen.'

Christie laughed. 'I'm just looking out for my boys,' she said lightly. The mood in the small car changed after she'd spoken and they spent the rest of the journey home in awkward silence.

Chapter 4

Christie was glad they enjoyed the meal she'd prepared. After arriving home from the funeral, Garrett and Connor had suddenly seemed exhausted and sad all over again. She'd suggested they go take a nap and rest a while. They'd been drawn back to the kitchen a couple of hours later by the smell of food.

'Wow, that's it. You can never leave again.' Connor laughed, mopping up the last of his sauce with a hunk of bread. 'You have to stay and feed us.'

'It's only lasagna.' She was playing it down but watching them devour the simple meal she had prepared had made her feel good. It surprised Christie to realize how much she still cared about every facet of their wellbeing, from how they were feeling right down to whether they'd had a decent dinner.

'It tasted great,' Garrett added, rubbing his taut stomach as he leaned back in his chair. 'Didn't realize how hungry I was.'

Christie thought they had coped amazingly well with the loss of their father. 'It's been a long time coming,' Connor said when she told them. 'We did our grieving long ago and over many months as we watched him waste away.'

'Amen to that,' Garrett added. 'Mom has been our main concern recently.'

They toasted Winton's memory over a glass of wine, each taking a moment to say goodbye in their own way.

The guys insisted she go relax in the living room while they cleared away the dishes, giving her a glass of the wine to take with her. Christie sank into a large leather sofa, avoiding the chair she knew had been Winston's. Thinking of him again made her sad and she took a long sip of her drink to chase away the feeling.

She'd only been in Catron County for just over 24 hours and already she felt at home, as if she had never left. If she was honest with herself, Christie would have to admit that every part of her wanted to stay. There was nothing back in Albuquerque for her now. Her parents didn't live anywhere near her home and she'd had to cope with her sham of a marriage alone. Christie wasn't angry at them but couldn't shift the feeling that their financial mismanagement had robbed her of her heritage. She'd been born in the family home that lay just over the hillside out of view, and she hadn't yet managed to bring herself to visit it. The sense of loss was too great. When the bank had repossessed her home, they had robbed her of far more than property. They'd taken her destiny too.

As Garrett and Connor walked back into the room, she wondered which of the men would have been her husband. As crazy as it seemed, Christie didn't have a clue. She'd loved them both. Still did, she realized with a jolt. Just the few hours she had spent with them had brought every emotion she'd ever felt crashing back. The connection had never been broken, at least not for her.

'What are you thinking about?' Garrett asked, smiling down at her softly as he refilled her glass.

'Being here again. It's so strange but it feels like I never left.'

'It doesn't feel that way for us Christie. There has always been a huge hole in our lives that only you could fill.'

'Don't say that, Garrett.'

'Why not?'

Christie put her glass down. 'Because you guys have done nothing but put pressure on me since I arrived, acting as if your whole happiness depends on how I respond to your crazy offer. You want me to stay here with you—both of you—and God help me, but I've been considering it.'

'Glad to hear it,' Connor said with a smile. 'What's the problem?'

'The problem is what kind of woman would that make me?' She laughed as the absurd thoughts she'd been having spilled out of her mouth. 'You don't even know me anymore. The person you want is the naïve little kid who thought you two were gods made flesh. I've grown up, Connor, and I need a grown up relationship.'

'That's what we are offering.'

'Have you thought it through? I mean, really? I've never even had sex with either of you yet you want me to commit to having a relationship with *both* of you. Do you realize how insane that sounds?'

Connor blew out a frustrated breath and Garrett paced away, running a hand through his hair as he thought on her words. Finally, he turned to her. 'Look, I admit the conversation went too far last night. I was putting the cart before the horse.'

'You can say that again,' Connor said accusingly.

'All we really want is a chance to see if what we believe is true.'

'And what's that?' she asked.

'That we are meant to be together. All of us.' Garrett sat beside her on the sofa, clasping her hands in his. 'Your entire childhood, you spent every waking moment with me and Connor. You were taken away from us at a time when we'd been fighting to keep our distance because we thought it was the right thing to do. Now, we want another chance to make things turn out the way they should have all along.'

'You don't have to say yes, Christie,' Connor added, taking the seat on her other side. 'But we think you feel the same way about us.'

'What do you mean?'

'Tell Garrett you don't love him.' Connor eyes fixed on hers as he dared her to speak the words.

'You know I can't,' she said finally, dropping her gaze. She heard Garrett let out a shaky breath beside her but she couldn't bring herself to look his way. A pulse beat loudly in her ears, drowning out the tense silence in the room.

'Ok, then tell me.' Christie stared at Connor again, angry almost that he could see through her so easily. She wished she could tell him that she didn't love him just to wipe the smug look off his face but she couldn't. Tears pricked her eyes as she shook her head slowly, letting him see that she was no more able to say it to him than she had been to Garrett.

'So where does that leave us?' he asked gently. Garrett remained silent, seeming content to let Connor speak, knowing his cousin had a way with words, Christie guessed. 'We are adults and we love each other. Why aren't we together?'

'I don't know. It's just wrong I guess.'

'Who says so?' Garrett asked finally. 'Who better to make the rules for our own lives than us?'

'All we are asking for is a chance to show you how great it could be,' Connor added when Christie fell silent again. 'Let us show you how much we love you, Christie.'

She sighed, sinking back against the sofa as she closed her eyes. Christie could feel them waiting for her answer. When they put it the way they had, their suggestion didn't seem unreasonable but she simply couldn't shake the idea that it was wrong. She told them so.

'Just let it go,' Connor soothed, leaning closer as the hand that had been smoothing her hair began to trail down over her cheek. He tilted her chin, giving her plenty of time to pull away as his mouth lowered to hers.

Christie gasped as their lips touched, self conscious at first to be kissing him in front of Garrett until she became aware of his hand on her shoulder. Almost as soon as she felt it, he turned her towards him and away from Connor, replacing his lips with his own.

Garrett's kiss seemed deeper and more possessive, as if he was trying to claim her. She began to respond to the probing of his tongue as it forced its way into her mouth. A long dormant ache came to life in her groin, and she tested the sensation, pushing against it as she realized how aroused she'd become.

Connor's hand caressed her thigh and she felt him move closer. His other lifted her hair, giving him access to her neck. Christie felt a hard jolt of desire slam through her as his lips found her skin and he nibbled at it gently. Garrett's free hand grasped her other leg and he wrapped a large palm around it, squeezing and smoothing as he made his way nearer and nearer to her crotch. Christie felt the first, fleeting pressure against her pussy as his knuckles grazed the fabric between her legs. Her insides contracted and she felt her muscles quiver at the warm, wet sensation his touch had caused.

'Stop,' she said weakly, ripping her mouth from Garrett's and pushing them both away. 'I can't think with the two of you doing things to me.'

The men stayed put but didn't touch her. Christie looked from one to the other. Two pairs of blue eyes stared back, watching as she straightened her clothes and got to her feet. Connor slumped forward to rest his forearms on his thighs, raising his head to look up at her. Garrett fell back, his chest rising and falling rapidly as he breathed heavily. His erection was clearly outlined in the denim of his jeans and she had to resist the urge to drop to her knees and release it.

'So, what's it gonna be, Christie?' he asked quietly, drawing her attention back to his face. 'If you keep looking at me like that, the choice isn't gonna be yours for much longer.'

'I can't have sex with both of you at once,' she protested weakly, knowing that she very much wanted to.

'That night back in the barn, we all started something we've just got to finish,' Connor said, getting to his feet to stand in front of her. 'None of us can move on until we do.'

'Besides,' Garrett added, 'it would cause too much jealousy if you chose one of us over the other. That's why we agreed, if it ever happened, it was gonna be all or nothing.'

'What makes you think I could handle that?' Christie asked

'It wouldn't have to be this way every time,' Connor said. 'Just this first time—then we'll see what happens.'

'This isn't just about sex,' Garrett said, getting to his feet to stand in front of her beside Connor, 'but I've had a hard-on for you for fifteen years and I can't wait another minute to fuck you and I know he feels the same.'

Christie got wetter. Garrett didn't know how to sweet talk a girl but if the look in his eye was anything to go by, he sure knew how to make her feel wanted. Her breath caught in her throat as she looked up at the pair of them. Every fantasy she'd ever had could be about to unfold in front of her and for the first time, she acknowledged to herself that it was exactly what she wanted. The damp throbbing in her pussy could not be ignored any longer.

She took a step back, enjoying a brief moment of power as she saw a fleeting look of disappointment cross their faces. 'Give me five minutes and then come up to my room.'

Chapter 5

Christie found she was excited and nervous as she took a quick shower and leapt into bed to wait for them. Jumping out again, she crossed the room on tiptoe, flicking off the main light, unsure she could take having two pairs of eyes she knew so well on her naked body. Changing her mind again, she put on a nightshirt and got back in to bed, then sat up with a laugh and took it off.

'Why the fuck am I so nervous?' she asked the empty room. Christie giggled breathlessly as she finally settled on staying naked and leaving the lights off.

A gentle tap at the door made her heart leap into her chest. 'Who is it?' she called, almost slapping herself in the head with a palm as she heard the idiotic words come out of her mouth. The sound of deep laughter from the other side of the door made her cheeks burn. 'I mean, come in.'

'Whaddya mean, 'who is it'?' Connor teased, poking his head around the door. Christie was glad she'd turned the light off and they couldn't see her cringing at her own silliness.

Garrett followed Connor in through the door, walking around to stand on the opposite side to his cousin. 'Do you mind if I open the drapes, Christie?'

'No, that would be nice,' she said, realizing it would be the perfect solution to her quandary. She wanted to be able to see them but not feel like she was on display herself. The moonlight would be just bright enough.

All rational thought flew from her mind as clothing started to hit the floor. Garrett's shirt landed first, followed by his jeans, leaving him in boxers that barely contained his erection. Connor decided on ripping off his bottom half before lifting his arms and pulling his t-shirt up over his taut abdomen and wide shoulders. His hard-on jutted forward proudly as he took a single step and drew back the sheet to get in bed beside her.

He kissed her gently on the lips, keeping his hands to himself for the moment as if giving her time to relax…but she couldn't. Christie became aware that Garrett had still not moved and she turned to find him standing uncertainly above them. If she didn't know him better, she'd have thought he was nervous. Christie put out a hand, inviting him to join them. A smile of relief crossed his handsome face and she realized that he needed to be sure that this was what she wanted. He shed his boxers revealing an erection slightly larger and thicker than Connor's—similar to the difference in their physiques—and took her hand as he climbed in beside her.

'We're gonna need a bigger bed,' Connor said. His voice trembled slightly, giving away that he wasn't as confident as he'd first appeared. Christie was relieved they seemed as nervous as her, in a way. While a huge part of her needed them to take control, another wanted it to be as special for them.

Garrett hushed his cousin, turning Christie's face towards him and kissing her deeply, rekindling the fire they had started in the room below. Her body reacted instantly, muscles clenching and releasing as her pussy cried out to be penetrated.

Connor's hands began to wander, pushing the sheet off her and cupping a breast to hold it steady as his hot mouth closed around her aching nipple. Christie started to shake as his lips continued downwards and his tongue circled her belly button before traveling further south. He pulled a leg towards him possessively, parting her to the night air that felt cool against her hot, sensitive skin.

Garrett continued to kiss her, brushing over her other nipple with an idle thumb and gasping as she bit his lip when Connor slid a long, thick finger inside her. Christie's hands went up into Garrett's hair and she held his mouth against hers as his cousin continued to slide his fingers easily in and out of her throbbing, wet cunt.

'My God,' Connor said, his voice breaking, 'I want to be inside you, baby.'

'Not yet,' Garrett warned, scooting down the bed and pushing Connor to one side. Garrett groaned as he watched Christie grinding in frustration against the loss of Connor's fingers. 'Hold on, darlin'. I'm gonna make you feel better.' He dropped his head and sucked her clit into his mouth.

Her body cleared the mattress at the touch of his lips, only to meet Connor's, coming to lean over. He straddled her torso, keeping his weight on his knees as he brought his groin level with her face. Christie grabbed his cock greedily, opening her mouth for him before he had a chance to ask.

'Shit!' Connor's hands slammed into the wall above the bed as she sucked on him hard and without warning. His head fell forward and he looked down at her, his mouth going slack as she drew the fight from him. Christie's hands found the taut muscles of his ass and she sank her nails into it as Garrett's lips on her clitoris began to pull her orgasm nearer.

'You are so fucking wet,' she heard him groan from his position between her shaking thighs. 'I'm gonna make you come so hard,' he warned. Pushing a thumb into her swollen pussy, he frigged her in time with the movements of his tongue.

Christie's insides began to coil tighter and tighter and she felt her muscles clamping down on the digit plundering her. A new sensation joined the others as the tip of Garrett's finger probed her anus. Her hips left the bed and he slid his free hand under her butt to keep her groin level with his face. His head began to move from side to side in rapid, jerky motions and Christie finally began to come.

Her thighs closed around Garrett's bristled face and she felt her pussy draw his thumb even deeper inside her when wave after wave

of spasms became hard, almost painful shudders as the orgasm drew
to its end.

Her body began to still and she realized she was no longer holding
Connor's dick. He still kneeled above her but had stopped to watch
her face as she came. Her eyes cleared to find him smiling down at
her and she gave him one in return.

He moved to lie at her side again, helping to roll her over onto her
front as Garrett put her on her knees. 'Are you ok?' he asked,
smoothing the hair away from her flushed face. Christie could do no
more than nod as Garrett's thick cock slid into her moist, hot pussy.

His animalistic groans echoed off the walls and spurred her into
action, sending her reaching for Connor again. He slid his body under
her shoulders, helping to brace her arms on either side of his hips.
Christie took his penis into her mouth again, determined this time she
would make him come. Poor Connor had been so patient and kind,
she felt almost guilty.

Garrett lifted her hips from the bed slightly, deepening the angle.
Tears pricked her eyes as he buried his hard, thick shaft into her over
and over again. Once more, Christie could do no more than hang on to
Connor blindly, unable to give him what she wanted as Garrett jerked
her body forward with almost brutal thrusts.

'Fuck me,' she said brokenly as the warning tremors began in her
groin. 'I want to come again…make me come.'

'I can't hold on….' Garrett's words died in his throat as his
orgasm began. Thick fingers bit into her hips as he slammed into her,
groaning her name between curses as his body jerked helplessly.

'Connor,' he said hoarsely, gesturing that he should take his place
before he fell away to the side, panting heavily as sweat coursed down
his body.

Christie was flipped onto her back by the younger cousin who
began to kiss and fondle her breasts as he slid inside her. He groaned
low in his throat as he sank his prick into her and began a slow,
persistent rhythm. Beyond the point of gentle lovemaking, Christie

lifted her knees, reaching down over his back and urging his ass into her harder, faster.

Never slow to take a hint, he brought her legs up over his shoulders to spread her wide and began to pound down into her. Christie's head jerked wildly from side to side as the angle bought her clit into to contact with his hard pelvis, just enough to make her moan but not enough to finish her off a second time.

Garrett moved to lie at her side and slipped a hand in between them, holding the flesh of her nub between the flat of his fingers and rubbing it briskly. His mouth found her breast and he flicked at her nipple, stopping occasionally to urge her onwards and tell her how beautiful she looked. Christie's fingers dug into the flesh of his arms, her nails making angry red marks as she clawed at him.

'Oh God, she's coming,' Connor groaned suddenly, launching into his own orgasm almost as soon as he'd uttered the words. He turned his head, sinking his teeth into the skin of her calf as she began to grind against the sensation of the hard cock penetrating her and the fingers rubbing her clit. Any thoughts she might have had that Connor would be the gentler of the two disappeared as his thrusts became hard, sharp stabs and he jerked wildly above her until the climax robbed him of his strength.

Her second orgasm hit more intensely than the first, brought on by the combined attentions of the two men. Christie was the one who swore this time, calling their names as they made her body nearly tear apart with the intensity of it all.

Connor brought her legs down quickly, as soon as she had calmed, as if he knew they would be sore. He stayed on top of her for a while longer, kissing her face and smoothing her hair from her sweaty brow. Garrett remained on his back beside them, linking his fingers through hers as he waited for them to catch their breath.

Christie gave Connor a gentle nudge with her hips, showing him she needed some space. He rolled away and Garrett took the opportunity to pull the sheet up over her, kissing her on the cheek and then getting to his feet.

'We're going to leave you to rest,' he said, gesturing to Connor that he should get up too. 'He's right, that bed isn't big enough for all three of us.' He reached down to grab his clothes, bunching them in his hand as he leaned over to kiss her again. 'Besides, mom is coming over in the morning.'

'You have no idea how much this meant to me, to us,' Connor said at the doorway as the pair left the room. Christie's eyes began to drift shut as pure exhaustion washed over her. The last thing she remembered was seeing their bodies silhouetted in the light from the hall and the gentle click of the door as it closed.

Chapter 6

Christie creaked open a reluctant eyelid to find Connor and Garrett standing over her—one holding a breakfast tray, the other a bunch of wildflowers.

She laughed. 'Am I ill?'

Connor smiled but Garrett didn't get the joke. 'What do you mean?'

'Nothing. I was teasing about getting breakfast in bed. For a moment, I thought I'd woken up in hospital.'

'Oh yeah, that's funny,' he said, smiling awkwardly and avoiding her eyes. Christie wondered what had made him so edgy. He'd gotten what he claimed he wanted the night before. Why was he acting so strangely now?

'What time is it? Did I miss your mom?'

'She's not coming out. Aunt Claire called and asked us to come over to her place instead. Apparently Mom wants to talk to us about something,' Garrett said.

'Which is why we brought you breakfast. We have to leave so we just came up to say goodbye.' Connor placed the tray on the nightstand. 'Relax and we'll see you later, ok?'

Garrett placed the flowers on her lap, dropping a shy kiss on her cheek and striding from the room without looking back. 'What's up with him?' she asked.

Connor turned to look at the empty doorway. 'Dunno. He's been like it since he woke up.'

'You don't think he regrets last night?' It made Christie's toes curl that she had to be the first to mention it but Garrett's behavior was worrying her.

'No way,' he said emphatically. 'I told you, honey. Last night meant everything to us.' He perched on the edge of the bed and wound a strand of dark hair around his finger. 'What about you? How do you feel this morning?'

She tried to keep the grin off her face but she couldn't. 'I've felt worse,' she giggled, squirming away when Connor poked her in the ribs.

A serious expression crossed his handsome face and he dipped his blond head. 'No kidding this time, ok? How do you feel?'

Christie saw the look of hope in his eyes and realized what had been wrong with Garrett. Both of them were waiting to see what her reaction would be. 'I feel loved, and cherished, and very, very lucky,' she said. A lump formed in her throat at the expression on Connor's face. His relief was evident but she could see he had more to say. However, the sound of Garrett's voice from below telling him that they had to leave made the words die in his throat.

'Best not to keep the big guy waiting.' He laughed. He got to his feet and leaned down to receive the kiss she offered him. It was sweet and fairly chaste considering what had passed between them already but it felt good. Connor made her feel like a kid on prom night. 'We'll talk later, ok?'

As she heard them drive away, Christie looked down at what they called breakfast—black toast, cold lumpy eggs and coffee. She picked up the cup and ignored the rest. As she drank the not-too-bad coffee, she tested the idea of actually staying with them on for size.

Her mind replayed every moment of the previous night in excruciating detail, making her blush. She'd always thought sex was over-rated—or that those who said they'd had mind-blowing experiences were just plain lying—but she didn't anymore. The sex she'd had with Garrett and Connor would have been amazing individually but together? Between them, they had ruined her for anyone else. Christie couldn't believe that she'd ever be truly satisfied with one man again.

There was much more to it all than just the physical pleasure of having two hot, sweaty men working hard at giving you an earth-shattering orgasm. The glow of love she had felt from both of them had made it even more life changing and she knew she would miss it every moment.

It seemed insane to even consider packing up her whole world and moving to the ranch with them but, what did she have to lose? Work wasn't an issue. Anybody could do her job and they would have no trouble replacing her.

She'd gotten the house as part of the marriage settlement, so it wasn't as if she would have to give up everything. If things didn't work out, she could just move back to Albuquerque. She sure as hell needed to put some distance between herself and Jack and being back in New Mexico with two big cowboys looking out for her would soon sort out that little problem.

And, God but she missed her home. Not the house that her family had lost so much as living where her soul wanted to be. Catron County was where she had been born and she longed to live and die there. Now, she had another reason to come back. Or should that be two?

* * * *

'What would you tell your mom?' she asked the boys later as they ate another meal she'd prepared. Christie had pretty much accepted that she would starve unless she cooked herself. Nothing they'd come up with so far had been anywhere near edible.

They got the gist of her question, making it obvious that the subject of her staying was as on their minds too. 'We've told her already,' Garrett said, shoving a big piece of steak into his mouth.

'What?' Christie almost dropped her fork. What the hell had they said?

'Calm down,' Connor said, seeing that Garrett couldn't answer with a mouthful of meat. 'All we told her was that we'd offered you a place to stay and a job.'

'How did she react?'

'She seemed relieved I think. I had a feeling when we went over today that she wanted to tell us that she'd decided to stay with Aunt Claire but didn't want to have to leave us to fend for ourselves. Garrett told her not to worry, that we'd asked you to stay, and if you didn't agree, we'd find someone else.'

Christie felt indignant. 'Find someone else? I didn't realize you could replace me so easily.'

'Only in the kitchen, darlin'.' Garrett winked at her as he spoke, making her smile right down to her toes. Still, the thought of anyone taking her place made her uneasy.

After clearing away the dishes, Christie took a deep breath and told the guys that she was going home the following day. 'Why so soon?' Connor asked earnestly. Garrett had gone quiet, trying to read her eyes as he waited for her answer.

'Because I need time to think,' she said, rubbing Garrett's shoulder in an attempt to ease the tension causing him to sit rigidly in his chair. 'And, if I still feel the same way I do right now, I need time to pack.'

'So you're thinking about saying yes?' Garrett spun in his seat, looking up at her with an expression that near broke her heart. She'd begun to feel as if she was solely responsible for their happiness and it gave her pause.

'You are gonna say yes, aren't you?' Connor pushed her for an answer when she fell silent again.

'Maybe.' She smiled, trying to chase the crestfallen looks from their faces. 'Guys, I gotta ask. What will you do if I say no?'

'Well, I can't speak for Garrett,' Connor said with a devilish gleam in his eye, 'but I'd probably throw myself in the canyon.'

'I'd stand in front of a stampede,' Garrett said dryly, exchanging a sly grin with his cousin.

'Very funny,' Christie laughed despite her embarrassment. She'd been seriously worried about their feelings and yet here they were teasing her about it. But their joking had put things into perspective. They'd be ok whatever her decision.

'I told you last night, all we ever wanted was a chance to tell you how we felt,' Garrett said, returning to his usual, down-to-earth self. 'If you don't want the same thing as us, that's fine. At least now, we will know for sure.'

'And nothing can ever spoil what happened last night,' Connor said, fixing her with an intense stare. 'You don't know how long I have wanted to be with you that way, Christie.'

'I exorcised a few demons myself,' Garrett added, voice low. Christie felt her insides tighten as the atmosphere in the room went from warm and friendly to hot and heavy in seconds. He cleared his throat as if refocusing his mind. 'What time do you have to set out in the morning?'

'First thing.' Christie could barely speak. The men became silent and still and she knew what they were thinking about. The tension of waiting to see if it would happen again was killing her.

'Um, we've been talking,' Connor said, his voice cutting through the electrically charged air. 'It might be a good idea if we spent some one-on-one time with you before you left—if that's ok?'

'But I'm leaving tomorrow,' she said coyly, realizing as she heard the words come out of her mouth that they sounded like an obvious come on. 'There won't be time.'

'Then let's not waste any,' Connor said, getting to his feet.

Chapter 7

'At least let one of us drive back with you,' Garrett insisted, refusing to let go of her overnight bag as she tried to put it in her car the next morning. 'That's a hell of a long way to go alone.'

'I made it here ok, didn't I?' She wrestled the bag from him finally, using her body to move him out of the way so she could close the trunk. 'Besides, I thought we agreed no pressure. The last thing I need is one of you there trying to influence my decision.'

Connor stepped in to help out. 'Let her go, Garrett. It's not like we'd ever be able to decide which one of us should get left behind anyway.'

Garrett dropped his arms, giving in for the time being. 'Ok, but phone us as soon as you get home. Just to let us know you are safe,' he added quickly when he sensed she had misunderstood. 'Even I don't expect you to make a decision that quickly.'

Christie tried to kiss the concern from his face, holding his unshaven cheeks between her palms. 'Stop worrying, big guy. I'll be fine.'

Connor gave her a tight hug and then opened her door for her, closing it with a pat as if to check it was shut properly. 'Don't keep us waiting too long,' he said, leaning in to kiss her cheek again before stepping back to join his cousin.

She pulled away slowly, straining to see them in the rearview mirror, watching as Connor placed his hand on Garrett's shoulder, as if to reassure him. Christie almost stopped the car and ran back to promise them both that she would return as soon as she could and never leave again, but she knew it wouldn't be true, not yet. Time and space to think was what she needed, despite the fact that every fiber of her being didn't want to go.

Once the road had taken her out of sight of the ranch, her mind started to drift back over her 'dates' with the men on the previous night. She was a little embarrassed to admit that she'd been disappointed to discover that neither of them intended to make the most of having her all to themselves. They'd been perfect gentlemen—dammit!

Connor had taken her for a sunset ride through the fields surrounding the house, telling her of their plans for the future and the struggles they faced in the current economic climate. 'If you decide to come live with us, the house and administrative side will be your main duties,' he'd said. 'Of course, we'd make you a full partner.'

'That wouldn't be necessary.'

'Don't be so quick to reject the idea, not until you've heard it all.' And with that, he'd begun to explain the plan he and Garrett had come up with to buy Christie's now derelict family home. 'We thought of running it as a dude ranch for paying guests. It wouldn't be the same as living there but at least it would be back in the family.'

Christie had been so overwhelmed at what he was suggesting, she'd been unable to reply. 'I know It's a little unfair of me to sweeten the pot and try and influence you,' Connor had said after telling her not to make a decision straight away, ' but I just wanted to show you how serious we are about this whole thing.'

Garrett had picked up where his cousin left off, using his part of the evening to drive her over the hill to the boundary of the property. 'I often come up here,' he'd said, pulling her into the crook of his arm as she'd begun to cry. 'I always picture you upstairs in that little room at the front, watching for us out of the window.'

Christie had laughed at the memory. 'You have no idea how many hours I wasted waiting for you guys. Ma used to say my face would get stuck to the glass.'

'So, have you thought any more on what you're gonna do?'

'Not yet, Garrett. This is all so overwhelming.' She'd struggled out of his arms then to pick at an imaginary piece of lint on her jeans. 'And, as much as I love the plans you and Connor have, it's just putting too much pressure on me.'

'I'm sorry. I know we promised, I just—'

'No, it's not that. What happens if things don't work out? Will I lose my best friends and my home? I couldn't go through that again.'

Garrett had forced her back into his arms, wiping the tears from her cheeks. 'Christie, don't you know us better than that? You could never lose our friendship, and as for the house, well, Connor and I have agreed that if anything happens you should retain full ownership.' After that, the talking had stopped for a while and they'd got nearer to making love than she and Connor had earlier, but Garrett had ultimately shown the same restraint as his cousin.

Christie squirmed in her seat as she thought about the two men and how easily she'd accepted the idea of being with them. Either of them alone would be enough for one woman. Connor was seductive, confident and devastatingly handsome. Garrett had enough raw sex appeal to fuel a rocket ship and a quiet, dependable manner that made you feel safe. Between them, they made the perfect man.

She turned off the interstate a mile from her home, amazed at how fast the journey could go if you had something to think about. She stopped a few blocks from the house to buy some fresh milk and groceries, and then pulled onto her driveway wondering why she'd bothered to come home at all.

It wasn't where she wanted to be.

Chapter 8

'You've got to be kidding me.'

Christie's best friend and work colleague, an outspoken woman in her early forties named Annemarie, looked at her as if she were crazy. Maybe she was right. She'd just told her about Connor and Garrett and their offer. 'What have I got to lose, Anne? It would get me out of this godforsaken place *and* away from Jack.'

Annemarie crossed her arms over her ample bosom, opening her brown eyes wide. 'But living with two men?' Her friend sounded scandalized, dropping her voice to a whisper in case anyone could hear them in the middle of the empty staff canteen. 'And what's wrong with this place anyway?'

'It's ok I guess,' she said, looking out of the window of the large office block she worked in. 'But spending my days sitting at a desk and dealing with middle management egos isn't quite how I imagined my life turning out.'

'But you imagined shacking up with two cowboys?' Annemarie tried to soften the harsh words with a smile. 'Has Jack fucked you up so badly that you have given up on love?'

'I do love them both, very much.'

'That's not love. It's a teenage crush you never got out of your system.'

Annemarie began to piss her off. 'Look, I am not asking you for permission. You are my friend and I wanted to let you know what was going on.' Christie began to regret telling her anything at all. 'It's real easy to judge other people when you have a good man at home.'

Her friend looked a little surprised at the fervor in her tone and Christie apologized instantly. 'I'm sorry. You must realize how lucky you are.'

'Sure do. I got me a fine man,' Annemarie said before changing the subject as if she realized it was almost exactly the wrong thing to say at that precise moment. 'Well, it certainly sounds like your mind is made up. Have you told them yet?'

Christie shook her head. 'No. I'm still not sure about the whole thing. I've been home almost a month and I'm still no nearer to making a decision than I was the morning I left the ranch.'

'So what's stopping you?' Annemarie gave her a searching look.

'I don't know—fear I guess. What if you're right? What if it is just something we all needed to get out of our systems?' Christie shook her head, unable to stop her thoughts spilling out now that she'd finally decided to talk to someone about it. 'What if they lose respect for me?'

Her friend clasped her hand, forcing her to look up into her eyes. 'Is that the problem or is it losing respect for yourself that worries you the most?'

'That too,' she said with a shaky smile. They fell silent, both lost in their thoughts as they realized they'd come to the real issue.

Finally, Annemarie spoke. 'Have they been in touch since you left?'

'No, that's another thing. What if they don't want me anymore after…you know.' Christie couldn't say it out loud.

'That isn't very likely, now is it? The one thing I know for sure from what you just told me is that they love you Christie. Ok, so I don't believe that three people can be happy in a relationship but I don't doubt for one moment that they are sincere.'

'Thanks, that means a lot.'

'That brings us back to you,' Annemarie said before looking at her watch and getting to her feet. 'Scratch that. We'll have to talk later. Lunchtime is over. I better get back to my desk. There's a big meeting scheduled for this afternoon.'

'Oh God, I totally forgot too,' Christie exclaimed, throwing the rest of her coffee down her throat and rushing out behind her friend. 'I don't know where my head is these days.'

She barely made it back to her desk in time, managing to prepare the notes and collate the information her line supervisor needed just as he arrived. From that point on, she had little to occupy her time and spent the remainder of the afternoon doing what she always did anytime she had a moment to herself these days—wondering what the hell she was going to do.

Why hadn't they been in touch? When she'd first come back, she'd been almost certain she knew what she wanted but, as the time had passed and she no longer had their seductive voices whispering in her ear, doubts had begun to creep in. Christie relied on their steadfast confidence to reassure her that she was doing the right thing.

An instant message from Annemarie popped up on her computer monitor. 'We'll talk more tonight. You cook dinner and I'll bring the wine, ok?'

Christie smiled, looking forward to going home that night more than she had in a whole month.

* * * *

As it turned out, they didn't get to open the wine. Annemarie had brought it as promised, but she'd also turned up bearing two of Christie's favorite indulgences—chocolate and a DVD of *The Way We Were*.

Christie groaned as the first strains of the film's enigmatic theme tune began to drift over her a few minutes later. 'God, I love this movie,' she said to her friend, popping a chocolate-covered bonbon into her mouth. The pair had piled onto the sofa after kicking off their shoes, ready to spend a couple of hours wrapped up in the gorgeous Hubble and his spirited Katie when the doorbell rang.

'Damn!' Christie leapt to her feet feeling uneasy.

'What's wrong?' Annemarie asked as she noticed that Christie hadn't moved to open the door. 'Aren't you going to see who it is?'

Christie shook her head. 'No. I've got a nasty suspicion it's Jack.'

'Is he *still* bugging you?'

'I thought he'd given up but obviously not.'

'Well, don't worry,' Annemarie assured, getting to her feet. 'I'll get rid of him. Nobody comes between me and Robert Redford.' She was still laughing as she stepped out into the hall.

Christie slipped into the bedroom to retrieve her purse and find the card with her lawyer's phone number. If Jack thought he could just continue to harass her then he was wrong. So help her, this time, she would get a restraining order against him.

'Christie, where are you?' she heard Annemarie call from the lounge moments before her head appeared around the bedroom door. 'You've got visitors.'

'What visitors?'

Annemarie stepped into the room excitedly, closing the door behind her for a moment as she spoke in a rushed whisper. 'Cowboys—two of them.' Her voice broke off into a giggle, and she clamped her hands over her mouth as she stared at Christie in wide-eyed admiration. 'Damn girl. You didn't tell me they looked like that.'

'Oh, so now that they're handsome cowboys, it's ok?' Christie had to laugh at her friend's behavior. Growing up in Catron County, men like the Wylers were ten a penny although not usually as good looking.

'Christie?' She heard Garrett's voice from the other side of the door getting impatient. 'Are you coming out or do we need to come in and get you?'

'Just a minute,' she called, giving her friend a look that told her she needed to pull herself together.

'Ooh, masterful too,' Annemarie said, still lost in her Wild West fantasy. Christie laughed and pulled her out of the way so she could open the door.

'Hi,' she said to the two irritated looking men filling her living room. 'Sorry about that. I…I was doing something.'

Her friend surged forward, one hand outstretched as she patted her hair with the other. 'Hi, my name's Annemarie. And you are?'

'I'm Garrett and this here is Connor,' he said as he shook her hand with a small grin.

'Pleased to meet make your acquaintance, ma'am,' Connor said, tipping the brim of his hat, playing the role of the gentleman cowboy to the hilt. Christie had seen them pull the same routine many times before and it always had the desired effect. Annemarie almost melted into a puddle right at their feet, giggling coquettishly.

'Christie's told me all about you.'

'Has she?' Garrett asked interestedly as he raised an eyebrow in Christie's direction.

'Hey, weren't you just leaving?' she cut in, ignoring Garrett's laugh as she gave Annemarie a look that told her to shut up.

'Was I?' her friend said, taking a moment to catch on. 'Oh, yes, I was.'

Outside a few moments later as Christie walked her to the car, Annemarie still hadn't calmed down at all. 'Forget everything I said before.'

'They just turned your head, that's all.'

'Well, damn. They are pretty head-turning.' She laughed before becoming serious. 'But really, Christie, they seem to care about you. Why else would they come all this way?'

'I guess so,' she said, hugging Annemarie quickly as she got into the car.

'Just don't do anything I wouldn't do,' she called as she drove away.

'Well, that narrows it down,' Christie said with a laugh as she turned back and walked into the house.

Chapter 9

'Do you have to try and knock every woman off their feet?' she asked as she walked back into the room. Christie found them occupying her sofa and picking their way through the open box of candy on the coffee table.

'What do you mean?' Connor asked, trying to look like the picture of innocence.

'Never mind.' She kissed them both on the cheek as they stood and pretended not to notice Garrett's lack of response. 'So, what brings you guys here?'

'Now, that's a stupid question,' Connor said, his natural good nature disappearing slightly. 'Did you forget you had the two of us waiting to hear from you?'

Christie blushed. 'No, I didn't forget. It's just that—'

'See, I told you we shouldn't have come,' Garrett said to him accusingly. 'She's obviously made up her mind and just hasn't bothered to let us know.'

'Hey, now just hang on a minute,' she protested, holding onto his arm to stop him stalking from the house. 'It hasn't been an easy decision to make.'

Garrett stopped, turning back to face her. 'So what part of it hasn't been easy? Is it that we care too much or just that we tried too hard?'

His anger took her by surprise. Luckily, Connor stepped in, forcing Garrett to 'sit down and shut up' before he took his turn to speak. 'Don't take any notice of him. He's not really mad, Christie. He's just hurt.'

'Why?'

'Because you haven't been in touch. We knew it would take a while but we kinda hoped you would be as excited about our offer as we were.'

'I was. I mean, I am.'

Connor began to look frustrated. 'So what's the hold up?'

Christie sat down on the edge of the coffee table, facing them. 'It's me. I've just gotten out of one relationship and I'm not ready to jump right into another one, especially not one as complicated as this.'

'Ok, well, I guess that's it,' Garrett said, looking angrily at Connor. 'Are you happy now?'

'At least we have an answer.'

'Yeah, the wrong answer. You pushed her and now she's not gonna come.'

Connor got to his feet, followed instantly by Garrett. 'Sure, we could have done things your way and stayed home getting more and more pig-headed.'

'Pig-headed?' Garrett's voice got dangerously low but Connor wouldn't back down, squaring up to the bigger man bravely.

'Yeah, I said it. Pig-headed.'

'Stop,' Christie yelled, leaping onto the coffee table to get between them. 'If you're gonna fight, you can both just get out.' Two pairs of eyes that had gone a cold, steely blue stared each other down for a moment longer.

'Well, he started it,' Garrett said, only serious for as long as it took for him to realize he sounded like a twelve year old. His face split into an unexpected grin.

'That was mature,' Connor teased, laughing openly. Christie joined in, relieved that the moment of tension had passed over. She'd forgotten the pair could fight at the drop of a hat. It was one more thing to consider.

'You gonna come down off that table?' Garrett said, picking her up before she could answer. He seemed reluctant to let her go and his eyes wandered over her body as his breathing got heavy.

'Put me down, Garrett.' She could have happily stayed in his arms, but first they had to talk. He placed her on the sofa and stood back next to his cousin. Christie took a deep breath. 'I will move back to Catron County,' she said carefully, holding up a hand to stop them saying anything until she'd finished. 'But on one condition.'

'Anything,' Connor said, fighting to keep triumphant smile off his face.

'What condition?' Garrett asked, cautious as always.

'On condition that I sell this place and buy back the family ranch in my own right.'

'So you won't agree to live with us?' Connor's smile got a little shaky.

'Not right away. My plan is to move back to the ranch and then we can take it from there.' The men looked at each other as one raised an eyebrow and the other shrugged.

'Ok, we can live with that,' Garrett said, 'but what about the rest?' Christie shook her head, unsure what he meant. 'You know—me, you and Connor.'

'Oh, that,' she said with a smile.

'Yeah, that.' Garrett's eyes made it clear he had the answer he wanted but needed to hear her to say it.

'Well,' she said, getting to her feet, 'I think I've forgotten exactly what it was you had in mind. You boys may need to refresh my memory.'

Chapter 10

Garrett pulled her trousers off over her feet and then stood to face her, letting his denim-clad erection graze seductively up her naked thigh as he did. Connor finished stripping off her t-shirt and bra and moved to stand behind her, pressing the crotch of his jeans against her ass, letting her know he was just as hard and ready as his cousin.

They'd moved straight from the living room into the bedroom without another word being spoken and, this time, she couldn't have cared if the lights stayed on or not.

Christie groaned and let her head fall back against Connor's shoulder as his lips found her neck while his hands slid up her torso to cup her breasts. Garrett watched her through slit eyes, biting his lip as his hand grazed over her abdomen and down over her pubic hair. She lifted her head to allow him to see her reaction as his hand sank into her moist curls.

Her legs shook as Garrett flattened his palm and pressed up into her flesh in a slow circular motion. Connor pinched her nipples between his fingers and thumbs and rolled them gently as his mouth moved to her shoulder. 'Fuck, she's so wet,' Garrett said to him, drawing Connor's gaze down to where his hand was buried.

She felt Connor move away briefly and heard him removing his clothing. Christie felt the wet head of his cock slide up the crease of her ass when he moved to stand behind her again. His hands went to the insides of her thighs, pulling her legs open slightly to allow him access. His teeth bit into her shoulder at the precise moment he slid a finger into her convulsing pussy.

Christie bucked back against him, forcing Connor to place a steadying hand around her waist as he continued to plunge in and out of her. Garrett leaned in to kiss her, sliding a tongue into her gasping mouth as his hand on her clit moved faster and faster. She dug her hands into his shoulders, needing to cling onto something solid as her knees began to shake and threatened to give way.

'That's it. Come for us, Christie,' she heard Connor say. 'I can feel the muscles in your cunt quivering. Just let it go.' Garrett dropped to his knees and replaced his fingers with his mouth, spreading her legs wide with his huge hands and sucking her clit.

Christie's orgasm slammed through her violently, making her body go rigid between them as neither man stopped his assault on her body. She began to grind her pussy into Garrett's face, trying to intensify the contact, clawing at the air wildly as she tried to find something to dig her nails into. Finally, they made contact with his hair and she clung onto it, holding on tight until the spasms subsided.

Connor slid his fingers from her, turning her around to kiss her face as Garrett stepped away to remove his clothing rapidly before moving up behind her again. Her arms were looped around Connor's neck and she tightened her grip as he lifted her legs from the floor and wrapped them around his waist.

'Put me inside you,' he groaned into her ear. Garrett put his palms under her ass and supported her weight as she dropped her hand to Connor's hard cock and positioned it at her entrance. The tip slid in easily, helped by the wetness of her pussy.

Christie's body quivered as Connor filled her when Garrett allowed her weight to drop onto the rigid penis. He took a step closer and began to lift her repeatedly, helping to intensify the impact of Connor's thrusts. Her hands found their way into his hair and she was forced to cling on again as Garrett continued to bounce her body up and down, helping Connor to ram his dick into her over and over again.

Garrett fingers closed over hers and moved her arms, forcing her to put them over her head and around his neck. His broad hands spanned her back, supporting her weight as she lay suspended between the two men with her head resting against Garrett's torso. Connor's hands went to her hips and he dropped his head in concentration when he was finally able to penetrate her as deeply as he wanted.

'Do you like Connor fucking you?' Garrett whispered into her ear. Christie groaned, unable to do more than nod.

Their words spurred Connor onwards and he looked up over her body with glazed eyes as his own peak began. 'Fuck!' he shouted, his cock sliding in and out of her rapidly until he impaled her one final time, jerking into her silently. He pulled out of her almost immediately, placing her feet back on the floor and dropping to his knees to suck in ragged breaths.

Garrett wrapped his arms around her waist, still standing behind her. 'Are you ok?' he asked.

Christie turned in his arms. 'I'm doing better than him,' she smiled, gesturing to the still breathless Connor now lying supine on the rug.

'Hey, I worked damn hard,' he protested with a weak laugh.

Garrett smiled and climbed onto the bed, beckoning her to him with a crooked finger. Christie crawled over his body, kissing his thighs, hips, abdomen and chest as she made her way slowly up to his mouth. Straddling him instantly, she lowered herself onto his cock, throwing her head back on a groan as she accommodated his larger size.

'Your pussy feels so fucking tight,' Garrett ground out as he began to jerk beneath her. 'Yeah, that's it.' He urged her on as she started to grind down onto his dick. He moved his legs, spreading his knees wide to push against her as she sank onto him.

Christie felt the bed dip beside her moments before Connor grabbed a handful of her hair and forced her to turn her face upwards to accept his kiss. His body pressed up against her side as he kneeled next to her, giving him easy access to her groin, stretched taut over Garrett's quivering abdomen. He placed his armpit over her shoulder and his thick bicep squashed her breasts as his fingers slid over her swollen clitoris. Connor's lips grazed the base of her neck as he alternated between licking and biting the soft skin.

'Keep doing that. She likes it,' Garrett groaned as Christie's body began to jerk around his hard cock. 'I can feel her pussy sucking on me.'

Christie opened her eyes just in time to see his orgasm begin. Garrett tried to hold her gaze but ultimately lost the battle, throwing his head back onto the pillows as his stomach began to convulse when his orgasm began. His hands locked onto her hips and he pumped her furiously up and down on top of him as Connor's fingers rubbed her hard. Her cries joined Garrett's as she followed him into her own climax, sinking her teeth into the hard shoulder inches from her face.

She collapsed on top of Garrett when Connor finally let her go, allowing him to fold his arms around her as they both gasped for breath. Connor lay beside them quietly, scooting over to the edge of the bed when Christie had to move.

'We're gonna have to take this bed with us,' he joked, lifting his head up to take in its full size. 'Why in God's name did you get one this big?'

'That's Jack's fault,' she said, still breathless.

'This was his bed?' Garrett sounded unhappy. 'We don't want it,' he said without waiting for her answer.

'No, he took his when he left but the room had been designed around a bed this size so I replaced it.'

'That's ok then,' Garrett said, chuckling as she pinched his arm.

* * * *

'So when are you coming home?' Connor asked as casually as he could an hour later. They'd just finished the meal Christie had been forced to offer them once she'd heard the sorry tale of how they almost starved while she was away.

'When are you guys heading back?'

'Is now too soon?' Connor's eyes shone with hope. Garrett, as usual, kept his emotions hidden but his body went tense, making it clear he was waiting for her answer.

'I guess not,' she smiled, as ready to start her new life as they. 'As long as you don't mind me staying with you until the ranch is ready?'

'Ok, but there's one condition,' Garrett said, finally allowing himself to smile.

'Yeah, what's that?' Christie played along, happy to allow him to think he was teasing her.

'You gotta bring that bed.'

THE END

Siren Publishing

Ménage Amour

Three
for the
Rodeo

Luxie Ryder

THREE FOR THE RODEO

Midnight Rodeo 3

LUXIE RYDER
Copyright © 2009

Chapter 1

'Do you think she would?' Kyle Johnson gestured with his dark head towards a woman at the other end of the bar. Hiding his face under the brim of his Stetson, he leaned his broad, heavy-set shoulders towards his friend.

'Who?' Gabe's green eyes scanned the crowd, landing instantly on the subject of the question. 'Hard to tell.'

'I bet she would.'

'Would what?' Sadie asked, unable to sit and listen to their conversation any longer without interrupting. 'What are you guys betting on now?'

'It's not a real bet, Sadie,' Gabe drawled. He turned to give her his full attention for a brief moment, blocking her view of the rest of the room with his tall, rangy body. 'Besides, you've made it real clear in the past that you have no interest in what Kyle and me do with the women we meet.'

She felt her cheeks redden. Damn him. Would he ever let it drop? 'Look, it's not a bad thing to tell two guys you work with that you are not going to fuck either of them, never mind both of them at the same time.'

Gabe hissed in an amused breath as Kyle nearly spat his mouthful of beer across the room. He wiped his face as he laughed quietly. 'Do you really think this is the place for that kind of talk, Miss Perkins?'

'Well, you were talking about it already,' she said defensively, refusing to allow their amused gazes to make her feel even more stupid than she did already. 'That's what you were saying, wasn't it? You asked if he thought that woman would go home with the both of you.'

The humor left Gabe's face to be replaced with the quiet watchfulness that was always there whenever she caught him looking her way. He held her eyes for a moment longer before dropping his head as he answered. 'Why do you care?'

'I don't,' she said, picking up her beer and turning her back on them before the conversation became even more personal. Sadie wished she'd never opened her mouth. It had only been a few days since she'd turned them down on their outrageous offer, and she guessed she'd just gotten her answer as to whether it was too early to test out if they were all still friends or not. They'd given her a wide berth since that night. Both guys seemed polite enough, but the camaraderie they'd shared seemed to have gone.

Sadie gave up trying to make friends with them for the time being and moved away to the other end of the bar. Not that either of them seemed to care. Their eyes had fixed firmly on the pretty little brunette who'd just noticed the two sexy cowboys watching her. The last thing Sadie needed was to watch Kyle and Gabe seduce someone right under her nose.

Sadie took a seat, determined to focus on the band playing that night and ignore the pair until they'd at least apologized for being so mean to her. She didn't have to wait too long before she felt a strong, heavy hand on her shoulder.

'Aw, don't be sore, honey. We're sorry.' Kyle sounded sincere.

'Ok.' She sighed, making room for them as they sat on either side of her. They fell into an awkward silence that lasted about as long as it took Gabe to swallow down the rest of his beer.

'What are you doing here anyway?' he asked. Sadie scanned the cowboy's green eyes for signs of the irritation she could hear in his voice yet he wore the expression of a guy simply asking a polite question. But with Gabe, nothing was simple.

'I missed you guys,' she said, trying to make her answer less revealing with a carefree shrug. 'I hadn't seen you since the night you…you know.'

'Yeah, we know.' Gabe smiled dryly. With his light brown, sun-streaked hair and sparkling green eyes, he looked nothing like the hard, sexy man she knew him to be. Gabriel P. Miles was one hell of a rodeo rider and one horny son-of-a-bitch when you got him fired up. Leading him on for fun wouldn't be a mistake she'd make again anytime soon.

Working at the permanent rodeo in Hurley, Colorado kept them all so busy that they only really saw each other if they made the effort. Her job involved grooming and taking care of the horses. It wasn't what she wanted, but she'd been lured into it by the promise of an opening for a woman rodeo rider eventually. The boss, Adie Phipps, had been evasive so far about when he actually intended to introduce the new event and the season was almost half over. But Sadie didn't mind too much. She loved her job and the town she worked in. Besides, she'd stretched the truth a little when they'd spoken for the first time. She'd never actually taken part in anything but the usual cowgirl events such as barrel racing or calf roping. Bull or bronco riding was something she'd planned to ask Gabe and Kyle to teach her about sometime soon, but she hoped she hadn't blown her only chance to get them to help her by acting crazy a few days earlier. Sadie doubted they'd be feeling very charitable towards her yet.

'It wasn't entirely our fault, you know,' Kyle said, cutting through her thoughts. 'I know we pissed you off by treating you like our kid sister, but it was your decision to up the stakes.'

'And we saved you from that guy,' Gabe reminded her gently. 'So we're not all bad.'

Sadie dropped her gaze. 'I know. I owe you both an apology, too.'

The guy he'd been referring to had pinned her against the wall as she tried to pass him on her way back from the bathroom. He'd stopped short of managing to kiss her but only because Kyle and Gabe had shown up.

'Are you sure you want another beer?' Gabe asked a little later when the conversation had finally moved on to safer ground. 'You've had a few.'

As relieved as she felt to be spending time with them again, Sadie just couldn't let them get away with treating her that way. If the price of admission back into their precious circle of friendship was that she had to allow them to monitor her every move, they could forget it. Kyle had been almost as bad as Gabe, looking at her with concern every time she lifted her beer bottle to her lips. Ok, so she'd been drinking a little fast, but she felt incredibly nervous.

'I'm not a kid,' she said with as much indignation as she could muster. 'And I don't need anyone watching out for me.'

'You're not a kid, huh?' Gabe said with a smile that didn't reach his eyes. 'Could have fooled me.'

'What do you mean?'

He dropped her gaze. 'Forget it.'

'No, I won't forget it. What do you mean?'

His bottle hit the bar hard, splashing beer over his wrist. 'You really don't want to hear it, lady.'

His anger surprised Sadie. She'd begun to think they had moved passed the awkwardness of what had happened between them but obviously, she'd been wrong. 'What in hell are you so mad about?'

'Oh, I don't know,' he said, his voice dropping to an angry whisper. 'Maybe it's the fact I was damn near inside you before you put an end to your little game the other night.'

'Things had gone nowhere near that far. I would never—'

'Never what? Never straddle my dick so hard that I could feel the heat from your pussy right through my jeans? Never groan and writhe on top of me so much that I could barely breathe before you decided that you couldn't see it through?' Sadie's cheeks flamed as Gabe fell silent. She watched a muscle tick in his jaw and knew he had more to say but he didn't get a chance.

To her horror, Kyle took over. 'He's right, Sadie. You played us both.' She shook her head in protest, but he raised a hand to stop her. 'The way you acted, we figured you were letting us know what you wanted.'

'Well, I wasn't. What kind of woman do you take me for?' She grasped around for something to fight back with. The way the pair spoke felt as if they blamed her solely for what had happened.

'I didn't take you for the kind of woman who made promises with her body that she had no intention of keeping.'

'All I did was get too drunk and have a little fun with you guys. It's not my fault you read too much into it.' The excuse sounded pathetic even to her, but she had no other explanation. 'Have a little fun' didn't even nearly describe what she'd done.

Gabe had growled a warning that she should behave herself but she hadn't listened, which is when the trouble had really started. She had leaned back against Kyle, moving her body across his hard abdomen and dipping and swaying in a way she could see drove him wild. She'd felt his cock get hard against her butt moments before his hands had snaked up her torso and cupped her breasts. The heat had slammed through her then—as it did again now—taking her breath away and she'd lingered a moment longer before common sense kicked in and she realized she had gone too far.

Sadie stared down at the table, feeling their eyes on her and the sexual tension the memory had caused. Her body throbbed and she shifted in her seat, almost groaning aloud at the dull ache in her groin. The seconds ticked by slowly as she sat under their scrutiny, refusing to look back at them.

Finally, Kyle spoke. 'Look, things just got out of hand. It's our fault for lying to you in the first place.'

'Lying?'

Kyle grinned. 'You seemed so sure you knew what Gabe and me got up to when we left the bar with a girl that we just played along. I guess I thought it was just a game at first, which is the reason I didn't set you straight. Then you started acting like some crazy, jealous female and that's when things got weird.'

Sadie didn't believe him. 'So you are telling me you and Gabe never, you know, shared a woman.'

Kyle's eyes flicked to the other man's as if deciding how much to say. He sighed. 'Once. It happened one time.'

'We shouldn't have teased you so much.' Gabe laughed. 'But you have to admit Kyle is right. You *are* a good girl deep down, no matter how hard you try to fight it.'

A couple of hours later, Sadie found herself tossing and turning in bed and thinking over what had happened. Kyle's words echoed through her brain. Maybe she was a good girl at heart. But why did it bug her so much that they thought of her that way? The label sounded way better than some a woman in her mid-thirties could have but for some reason, whenever they said it, it made her hackles rise.

She'd been drunk when she'd asked them why they often left with just one woman between them. Gabe and Kyle had been hitting the beer hard too, which is the only reason they told her the truth, she guessed. After she got over her initial shock, Sadie's alcohol-fuelled ego had come into play. 'So why haven't you ever asked me?'

Sure, she knew she looked like a slightly more feminine version of them, albeit six inches shorter. She wore a Stetson, jeans and a checked shirt the same as they did but with her curly hair usually scraped back into a low ponytail. But she knew other men found her attractive enough. She was an average 5'8" blue-eyed blond, made a little more unique by her strength and athleticism. Her body was toned and tan, and guys seemed to like it.

Sadie turned over in the bed and punched her pillow as she remembered how quickly the atmosphere had changed once she'd asked the question. Kyle had pinned her to the spot with one of his brown-eyed laser locks. 'You're too much of a good girl. We don't mess with good girls'.

Gabe had been kinder, sort of. He'd laughed dismissively, making it clear to her mind that he thought she couldn't handle what they had offered.

'You guys don't really know me. I can be wild sometimes,' she'd said.

'Not wild enough for us, Sadie.'

From that point on, she'd been determined to get a reaction out of them. There was a lot about her that they didn't know. Guys had been falling over themselves for years to get to her back home in Arizona. She'd loved and left a few of them, too. How dare Kyle and Gabe write her off so easily.

So, she'd begun playing with fire by leaning across them whenever she needed something, brushing against them at every opportunity and giving them her back every time the band played something fast and heavy, and she could use the music to wind her body sinuously in front of them.

By the time she actually stopped to see if her efforts were having any effect, she'd been relieved to see that Gabe and Kyle had their eyes fixed firmly on her. And what she saw in them told her that they had reassessed their opinions of her.

Problem was, they weren't the only men in the room watching her every move, which is how she found herself fighting off some guy on her way back from the bathroom. She'd been relieved to see Gabe and

Kyle appear out of nowhere and drag him away until they came back and dragged her away, too. With only a handful of years difference in their ages, the slightly older guys somehow made her feel like a little kid at times. She was a grown woman and it bugged the hell out of her that they refused to see her that way.

'Behave,' Gabe had growled, pulling her onto his lap, but she hadn't listened. He'd looked so stern and unbending that she'd been determined to get a reaction out of him, that was until she felt his 'reaction' pressing hard against the crotch of her jeans. Kyle's attempts to control her after she'd jumped off Gabe's lap hadn't worked much better.

'Stop it,' Kyle had shouted, grasping her by the shoulders and placing her on a chair, 'unless you plan to finish this somewhere private?'

Sadie had sobered up fast then. She'd looked at Gabe in shock, expecting him to put Kyle straight but he'd simply stared at her, as if waiting for an answer. She'd dropped his gaze to stare down at her lap, shaking her head in answer to the question.

'You're going home,' Gabe had said, grabbing her by the arm and leading her from the bar, followed by Kyle. The short walk to her apartment had been an awkward one. Both men had kept their distance and a stony silence, leaving her in no doubt that they weren't amused by her games.

'Look guys, I'm sorry I got a little carried away.' Sadie had tried to apologize when they reached her door. 'Come on in for a coffee. We can talk about it.'

'That's not a good idea,' Gabe had said quietly. 'We've all had too much to drink and things might get out of hand. Just go to bed, Sadie.'

With that they'd walked off, leaving her torn between feeling like she'd had a lucky escape and wanting to know just what might have happened. And in the couple of days since then, her curiosity hadn't waned.

Sadie felt glad she'd at least made the effort to talk to them in the bar earlier. There were many places to drink in town if she wanted to avoid a confrontation but she'd searched them out. She missed them. It was her first season at the rodeo and the guys were her only real friends. Or, they had been. Still, she felt relieved they had at least come to an uneasy truce.

For the first time in a few days, Sadie drifted off to sleep, looking forward to seeing them at work again.

Chapter 2

She looked for them again the following afternoon before the show, determined to build on the shaky start they had made on repairing their friendship the previous day. Sadie finally found them in the medical room. Gabe was getting a massage to help with the strain riding bareback every night for six weeks had caused, and Kyle got treatment for a graze to his head from working with a bull earlier.

'Hard day, guys?' she said cheerily, suppressing the fear that rose in her throat as she saw the blood on Kyle's shirt. How they got through each day without major injuries was a miracle to Sadie. Thankfully, the sport had changed in recent years and the organizers had finally learned they needed to take much better care of the talent, hence the qualified masseur and medical staff in the room with them.

'I'm doing better than Kyle,' Gabe said, groaning almost erotically as the strong hands of a statuesque therapist worked their way down his back. Sadie felt as much as heard the sound he made. He closed his eyes, biting down onto his lip as the woman continued to work over his oily, muscled skin. A pulse beat harder in Sadie's throat as she allowed her eyes to roam over his torso—from the dimples she could just see above the waistband of his jeans to the bicep muscles stretched taut around the sides of the table. Her face got hot and she shook her head to clear it. Why the hell did she react to the sight of him this way?

She turned away blindly, deciding it would be safer to focus on Kyle, only to find that he had been watching her reaction to Gabe. He hissed a little as the medic swabbed his wound and applied a couple of butterfly stitches but his eyes stayed on her. Shuffling from one foot to the other, Sadie fought the urge to run from the room as his gaze flicked down over her body. Already aroused by the sight of Gabe, she felt her nipples spring to life under Kyle's perusal. A half smile lifted the corner of his mouth as he pulled his bloodied shirt out of his jeans, tore the snaps open with a savage jerk and threw it to the floor.

Sadie felt her knees go weak. Unsure whether she had actually just licked her lips or not at the sight of his broad tanned chest, she cast a quick look in Gabe's direction and found his eyes on her ass. His gaze lifted slowly to hers, making it clear he didn't care that she'd caught him. His expression told her what she had already begun to suspect. Things had changed between them irreparably. They were no longer—could no longer—be simply 'friends'.

'How is your head this morning?' Kyle asked, breaking another awkward silence.

'Not as bad as you might think.' Sadie laughed. 'I told you I wasn't as drunk as you thought. I might give the bar a miss for a few nights though.' They didn't need to know that she'd just found another reason besides her health to avoid the place. She couldn't handle the sexual tension that seemed to spark into life every time they got together these days.

The door opened suddenly and Adie charged into the room. 'You guys ok?' he asked in his typical brusque, monosyllabic fashion. It took him a moment to notice Sadie. 'What are you doing in here?'

'She just came to check on us, boss. We don't mind.' Kyle leapt to her defense, stopping Adie from steering her out of the door by the firm grip he had on her elbow. The man was a giant—the best part of seven feet tall and almost as wide. Luckily, he had a gentle soul but you had to know how to handle him. Adie could be frightening at first glance.

'You'd better not be bugging them before the show,' he said to her then turned to Kyle. 'You gotta watch this one, she's always bugging my boys to teach her how to handle a steer or ride a bronco.'

Both men seemed shocked, but Gabe actually laughed out loud. 'Why in the hell would she want to do that?'

She put a hand up, waving at them in sarcasm. 'Stop talking about me like I'm not here.'

'I've been thinking about having a women's rodeo feature as part of the show. I took Sadie on believing she had more experience than she actually does,' Adie explained, giving her a hard look. 'Damn near fired her when I figured out she'd lied to me but her work is good and the horses are thriving since she's been taking care of them so I let it slide.'

'I can do it, Adie,' she pleaded, realizing that this was her chance to get it all out in the open and ask for the help she needed. 'I already know a lot. I just need someone like Gabe and Kyle to teach me the rest.'

'You want us to teach you?' Kyle said, his brown eyes getting hard and cold. 'Like hell we will.'

'W-what?'

'You heard him,' Gabe added, getting to his feet and shrugging his shirt on roughly. 'If you want to kill yourself, you can do it without our help.'

'Lots of women work the rodeo, why can't I?' she protested, taken aback by their reaction.

'Shit, Sadie. You don't weigh ten pounds wet. How the hell do you think you could handle a bull?'

'I'm stronger than I look. Besides, I've seen plenty of other women do it.'

'Yeah, well it's no fit job for them and definitely no fit job for you,' Kyle muttered, making to walk past her out of the room.

Shaking with emotion, she could barely spit out her words. 'Oh, that's right. I know from bitter experience what you guys think I'm good for.' Her eyes warred with theirs until she heard Adie clear his throat and realized she'd almost said too much.

'What in hell are you yakking about?' Adie bellowed, oblivious to the reason for the sudden rise in tension.

'Ask *them*,' she said, storming from the room and slamming the door as hard as she could.

Later that night, Sadie was drawn to the rail of the arena, no more than a few feet away from the livestock. She stood close enough to feel the chunks of dirt hitting her face, kicked up by the hooves of the animals charging passed. She could smell the leather and sweat, hear the grunts of the bulls and the curses of the riders trying to stay on them. As always, Sadie found the sights and sounds exhilarating if a little scary. Two thousand pounds of angry beef stampeded past trying to throw the rider off its back and everyone within close range felt the effects of its efforts.

Kyle just about managed to tame the wild beast beneath him. Sadie couldn't help but admire the way he rode and how totally in control he seemed. The dueling pair approached her side of the ring, and she stood back quickly. Many a bull kicked out at the crowd or pinned the rider against the rails in its rage.

Sadie knew it to be a dangerous sport but it didn't stop her wanting to find out if she could do it. She made a note to remind Kyle and Gabe how they would have felt if when they were growing up on ranches in different parts of Colorado, people had dismissed their ambitions so easily. From what they'd told her in conversation, Gabe's pa had been an ornery son-of-a-bitch who only had time for work and Kyle hadn't had a father around at all. Lucky for him, an older brother had become the patriarch and spent a lot of time helping his younger siblings achieve their goals in a way he never would.

Neither of them would be living the lives they did if somebody hadn't take the time to help them out and teach them a skill. Why, because she happened to be female, wasn't anybody prepared to do the same for her?

A flurry of activity followed as the bull managed to unseat Kyle and aim an angry foot at his head that luckily fell short of its target.

The clowns jumped into the ring, quickly distracting the beast as Kyle got to his feet, retrieved his hat and used it to brush the dust from his clothing.

Sadie felt sure he hadn't seen her watching until the moment he turned and looked her right in the face. His expression was one of challenge, as if daring her to match what he just did. The half smirk on his face made her hands itch with the urge to slap him and she seriously considered flipping him the bird. He turned and walked away before she could act on the impulse, leaving her with no choice but to stare at his retreating back in anger.

'Taking a master class?' she heard Gabe mutter into her ear. Whirling around, she smacked straight into his hard chest. Where had he come from and why in hell was he standing so close?

'I'm still not speaking to you,' she said, tilting her head right back to look him in the eye. 'Get lost.'

She began to turn her back on him again but he grabbed her arm and spun her around, pinning her against the railings and preventing her escape with a strong arm on either side of her body. 'Don't you think it's about time you grew up?' he said.

'Don't you think it's about time you stopped trying to tell me what to do?'

His jaw tightened and he leaned in so close she could feel his hot breath on her face. 'You know what's eating you, lady?'

'No, but I'm sure you're gonna tell me,' she drawled, rolling her eyes. 'Come on, big guy. Tell me what my problem is.'

His eyes went dark and he took a quick check left and right to make sure nobody could hear what he was about to say. 'You're just mad as hell we called your bluff the other night.'

Sadie gasped, stunned by his arrogance. 'Are you *still* going on about that? Just because you can't forget about it, don't assume I feel the same way.'

'Oh, I know you haven't forgotten Sadie. You wanted me and Kyle to see it through…to make you admit what you wanted us to do to you.' She shook her head, rejecting his words as her breath became shallow and her heart threatened to beat out of her chest. Gabe leaned in closer. 'You wanted us to fuck you every way we know how, but you just can't admit it.'

His husky voice trickled through her, taking a direct route from her ear to her groin. She felt her pussy convulse once, twice, and then a moist heat soaking her panties. Sadie shook her head weakly, closing her eyes against the sensations he had caused and unwilling to show him that he was right. Damn him.

'All I want from you and Kyle is some help with learning how to ride the rodeo.' She braced her hands against his chest and used her full weight to push him away, giving herself space to think and breathe again. 'And that's it.'

'I can't speak for Kyle, but there's no way in hell I'm teaching you anything that's liable to get you hurt.'

His mood changed so abruptly that it took her a moment to catch up. 'Fine, if you guys won't show me, I'll find someone who will. Not everyone is as sexist as you.'

'Sexist?' he roared. 'What in hell are you talking about?'

'Well, why else would you refuse to help me if it isn't down to some macho idea that women shouldn't work the rodeo?'

Gabe blew out a harsh breath, shaking his head in disbelief. 'You think you got it all figured out, don't you? Has it occurred to you that maybe we care enough that neither of us wants to be the reason you run out and break your damn fool neck?'

'Oh,' she said, at a loss for words. She hadn't considered that. Besides, since when had they 'cared'? Last she knew, they were just plain mad at her.

'You know, Sadie, for a smart woman, you can be real dumb sometimes,' Gabe said before turning and walking away.

Chapter 3

Sadie's work after a show involved mostly unsaddling the horses, checking them over for injuries and releasing them into the pen. Adie didn't use a stock controller for the animals due to the fact that, besides the very basic help he got from Sadie, he looked after the horses himself. They were insanely valuable and he wouldn't trust anything but the simplest of tasks to anybody else. She knew no special skill was required to do her job so she wondered as she threw some bales of hay into the stalls later that night, why he kept her around. Obviously her rodeo ambitions didn't come very high on Adie's list of priorities.

It was also obvious that she needed to keep her head down for a while. Things had gotten tense with the guys. Her encounter with Gabe earlier had knocked her off kilter. She'd seen him with many women but he'd never acted the way he did with her. Gabe had a laid back attitude to sex and treated his frequent successes with women in the same way he did his rare rejections, as if he didn't really care. Sadie had never seen him get so riled up about anything. Ever.

The subject of her thoughts and his ever present sidekick appeared in the stable doorway. 'Hey, Sadie,' Kyle said, running a hand through his dark hair.

'Hello,' she replied cautiously. The three of them hadn't had a normal conversation in over a week so their sudden appearance at a time when they should be in the shower or getting a rub down made her nervous. 'What's up?'

'Nothing much. Just thought we'd check everything was ok.'

Sadie studied the pair of them a little more closely. Gabe, who still hadn't spoken, had his eyes fixed firmly on the floor and Kyle had his hat in his hand. What in hell was going on? 'I'm ok. Busy as usual.'

'Gabe wanted to talk to you about this rodeo idea.'

The look Gabe gave Kyle made it clear he wanted to kill him, but he let it slide. 'We both did,' Gabe said.

Sadie wasn't buying. 'Do you mean talk to me or talk me out of it?' The silence that followed her statement gave her the answer. 'Well, don't bother. I know better than to ask you guys for help again.'

'Jesus, woman, why do you have to turn everything into a fight?' Gabe kicked a lump of dirt across the stable. 'We just wanted to explain why we don't want you to do it.'

'We realize we could never talk you out of it, but we want you to consider some things,' Kyle added.

Sadie sighed, biting back her irritation. 'Look, if you want to tell me it's dangerous, I know. I'm not asking for your approval. I just want some help.'

'So you don't care how we feel?' Kyle persisted.

'About this? No, I don't.'

'Seems to me you don't much how we feel about anything these days,' he replied, his jaw setting in a firm line.

Sadie spun around to face him, searching his eyes for a clue as to what he was talking about, as if she didn't know. 'Don't play games, Kyle. If you've got something to say, spit it out.'

'She's talking to us about playing games,' he said to Gabe, laughing at her openly. 'The woman who fucked with our minds and bodies and then pouted because she got the reaction she'd been trying for, is accusing us of playing games.'

His eyes glittered brightly and she could see Kyle fighting to hold on to his temper. Gabe put a hand on his shoulder to calm him down. 'We agreed not to mention that, remember?'

Kyle finally dropped her gaze to look at Gabe in disbelief. 'Why are you so calm? You're more pissed off than I am.'

'True. But I've been thinking about things and we need to find a way move on.'

'And how do you suggest we do that?'

Sadie swallowed hard. Gabe had leaned back against a stall with his thumb hooked into the waistband of his jeans. His shirt collar opened a little more and she could see the sweat glistening on his skin in the soft light of the stable. Kyle looked from one to the other as he put his hat back on, his face taking on a half smile, as he seemed to read what Sadie could see clearly in the other man's eyes.

'That's pretty much up to Sadie,' Gabe said to Kyle, all the while staring at her.

'What do you mean?' she whispered, battling to hear even her own words with blood pounding in her ears. Both of them had become quiet and watchful, trapping her between them with only their eyes. Sadie looked from one to the other and fought to calm the quivering that began in her abdomen. Her lips parted and she blew out a shaky breath as she tried to ignore the first, tentative throbs of arousal coursing through her body.

'You can make this right, Sadie,' Kyle said, picking up where Gabe left off as if by some unspoken command. 'You need to finish what you started.'

'You're both crazy,' she shouted, but not from anger. The surge of heat that vibrated through her pussy at his words shamed her. Sure, the idea had occurred to her many times since that night, but she always rejected it instantly as nothing more than a wild fantasy that almost came to life. She could never do it.

'Yeah, crazy like a fox,' Gabe drawled. 'I know what you want, Sadie, even if you won't admit it. Have you asked yourself why you've been searching us out these last few days?'

'I...I told you. I need help with—'

'You need help with something baby and it ain't learning how to ride a bull.' Gabe didn't smile to soften his words. His voice had lowered and the message was clear. 'You know what you need.'

Sadie felt the color rise on her cheeks and she prayed the reaction of her body wasn't showing on her face. 'Well, if I did need *that*, I certainly wouldn't be asking either of you.'

'Oh, is that so?' Kyle asked, taking a step nearer, drawing Sadie's attention to the crotch of his jeans. She bit her lip as she remembered how the impressive erection in front of her had felt against her ass when she rubbed against it. Kyle seemed to read her mind. 'Or do you need to show me again how little you want me?'

'Why do you keep talking about that night? I apologized for that,' she snapped, desperate to distract them from their obvious intention of making her admit she wanted it then and still did now.

Gabe laughed. 'No need to apologize, Sadie. Just stop fighting the inevitable.'

'You sure are one arrogant bastard.' She grabbed her pail and headed for the door, pushing Kyle out of her way as she passed.

She attempted to walk out before he could reply, but couldn't escape the sound of his taunting words. 'Honey, it ain't arrogant if I'm right.'

Chapter 4

It ain't arrogant if I'm right.

Those words had haunted her in the two days since Gabe had uttered them, but he didn't look anywhere near as smug now, Sadie thought with satisfaction. His face had set into a hard mask when he'd seen who she was with. Draping her arm over Billy's for added effect, she gave Kyle and Gabe the haughtiest look she could muster and turned her back.

She unwound her arm from Billy's when she saw his look of surprise. He was a sweet kid and she didn't mean to give him the wrong impression. He'd agreed to help her after she'd had to tolerate a load of the guys poking fun at her the other night as they waited to collect their pay from Adie's trailer. The news about her ambitions had spread like wildfire, probably aided by the medical staff that had been in the treatment room when Adie blabbed about it. Since then, she'd been teased and taunted about it to within an inch of her life. None of the men working the rodeo took her seriously anyway, and this latest tidbit of information about her ambitions hadn't helped.

Kyle and Gabe hadn't said a word, not even in her defense. Once or twice they'd told the guys to get back to work, but she guessed that wasn't for her benefit.

'So, when can we start?' She'd been nagging Billy since they hit the bar, but he'd been a little evasive. 'I can't tell you how pleased I am that you've agreed to help me.'

'Yeah, ok.' His unenthusiastic response didn't bode well. Had he changed his mind? An hour later, she knew for sure.

'Look, Billy. Maybe you got the wrong idea about exactly what it is I want from you.' Sadie slid out of the younger man's grasp. The 'sweet kid' had turned into a letch and she'd had enough of being pawed. The casual touch on her ass was the last straw. 'Get your hands off me.'

'Yeah, get your hands off her.'

Billy spun around, following Sadie's gaze to the angry cowboy suddenly standing behind them. Gabe looked about fit to explode, held back only by Kyle's hand on his shoulder.

Billy struggled to find his voice when confronted with the two much older and larger men. 'I...I was just being friendly.'

'Leave him alone,' she snapped, irrationally annoyed by their interference. 'I told you before, I can look after myself.'

Gabe's expression changed from one of concern to one of amusement. If she didn't know better, Sadie could have sworn he loved getting her riled up. 'Yeah, so I see.'

Silence hung between the foursome, heavy with the various kinds of tension swirling around them. Gabe looked deep into her eyes, and without warning she was right back to that night and almost as hot for him. Her eyes flicked to Kyle but he wasn't paying her any attention right at that moment. He had Billy pinned to the spot with a look that just about dared him to make a move. The younger guy dropped his head almost immediately, looking around for an escape route as he picked up his beer.

'Well, I guess I'll be turning in for the night,' he said as casually as his nerves would allow. 'Nice talking to you, Sadie.' The three of them watched him take a couple of careful steps backwards before turning and walking swiftly from the bar.

'Who the fuck do you think you are?' she asked as she turned on Gabe. 'I've got a daddy back in Arizona and I don't need another one.'

'You looked like you needed a hand, is all,' Kyle tried to explain, but she didn't let him finish.

'What is it with you guys these days? Why are you acting so weird all of a sudden?'

'We're acting weird?' Kyle repeated, his voice rising in disbelief. 'What in hell's name are you doing with that kid?'

'He offered to help me.'

'He sure looked keen enough,' Gabe added, still wearing the stupid half grin she'd begun to mistrust. His outwardly good humor didn't fool her for a second. His eyes were hot, burning bright with something she couldn't put a name to. Maybe he could sense the emotions swirling around inside her? His gaze locked with hers and she felt as if he could read her like a book. To her surprise, the knowledge that she was aroused seemed to irritate him. His green eyes went a shade darker moments before he spoke. 'What's up, baby? Is it easier to play your games with a boy than it is with a man?'

Sadie gasped. Gabe hated her. That was the emotion she could see in his face every time he looked at her. Maybe Kyle did too? 'That's not fair, Gabe.'

She felt the tears spring to her eyes despite her best efforts. Kyle winced then blew out a long breath as he dropped his head. Gabe tried to reach for her hand once he realized he'd upset her. She slapped it away.

'Aw shit, Sadie,' he said, his voice tinged with genuine regret. Sensing he was about to apologize, she picked up her hat and walked from the bar. She didn't need him or his pity.

An hour later, she turned over in bed and put the pillow over her head, trying to ignore them. Gabe and Kyle had been throwing small rocks at her window for a good ten minutes, trying to get her to answer. *Jesus*, she thought, *if they made any more noise, they may as well just smash the glass and be done with it.*

'What do you want?' she whispered angrily when she finally gave in and opened the main door for them a few minutes later. 'Haven't you two done enough damage for one night? Do you want me to get kicked out of my apartment, too?'

'Sorry.' Kyle stood in the doorway, almost obscuring the figure of Gabe behind him. 'Can we come in?'

'There's not much point whispering now,' she said with a sigh, gesturing that they should follow her into the apartment. A noise out in the hall that sounded suspiciously like her landlady opening her own door to see what was going on spurred her into action, and she dragged the men into the room quickly, hushing them with a finger pressed to her lips.

Pressing an ear against the frame, she strained to hear Mrs. Williams open the deadbolts on her own apartment door moments before the hinges creaked noisily, announcing her entrance into the hallway. The shuffle of feet stopped outside Sadie's apartment and she flapped a hand at the men frozen in the centre of her small room, gesturing that they should stay put and keep quiet. A giggle rose in her throat as she got an image of both her and the landlady with their ears pressed up against separate sides of the same door but she managed to suppress it. Finally, the footsteps moved away and the sounds of the hinges and locks being put back into place gave Sadie the all clear.

Turning to Gabe and Kyle, she wore a smile for the amount of time it took her to remember that she was upset with them, and to notice that they were looking at her funny. Ok, so she had her nightshirt on, but it wasn't indecently short, although she guessed they had never actually seen her legs before. It occurred to her that she wasn't wearing a bra either so she crossed her arms as casually as she dared.

'So, is one of you going to tell me what's so important you had to almost break a window? Well?' she repeated when they continued to stare at her.

'Sorry,' Gabe said, shaking his head. 'I just never saw you with your hair down before. It's real pretty.'

Sadie squirmed under his gaze, resisting the urge to run a hand through what she felt sure were messy, blonde curls. 'I'm damn sure you didn't come here at midnight to talk about my hair.'

'You're right. We didn't.' Kyle stepped forward. 'It does look real nice though.'

She put her hands on her hips to stare at them impatiently before realizing that the gesture brought their eyes down to her breasts. Sadie crossed her arms again, her patience and frayed nerves threatening to snap. 'Ok, that's it. Get out.'

'We need to talk,' Gabe said quietly. 'You know it too, Sadie. We gotta sort this mess out.'

Despite the nerves fluttering in her stomach at the prospect, she had to admit he was right. But if their past attempts at discussing what had happened were anything to go by, they couldn't risk starting that conversation in her apartment. Sadie nodded her agreement as she thought quickly. 'Ok, why don't you wait for me outside? We can take a walk or something.'

They left without another word and she found them on her doorstep as she stepped out into the warm night a few minutes later. The jogging suit she had thrown on over her nightshirt was about all she could manage in her nervous state. Her mind had raced over the possibilities as she had donned the clothing with shaking hands and she'd acknowledged to herself that there seemed to be only one way this could really end. She would have to leave town.

Kyle straightened up from his position leaning against the wall as she appeared. 'We thought it would be easier if we all just had a coffee at Gabe's place.'

'Is that ok?' she asked Gabe, more to try to feel out his mood than anything else.

'Sure. But I need more than coffee.' His eyes were unreadable where the brim of his hat shielded them from the glare of the streetlight but despite the laughter in his voice, she could see from his posture that he was far from relaxed.

They began to walk and Kyle made good use of the time, explaining to Sadie that they would never have started anything with her. 'But not for the reason you think,' he clarified, when he saw her bristle at the seeming putdown.

'We'd agreed that you were off limits,' Gabe added, stirred from his silence. 'When you first joined our outfit, we both wanted to make a play for you. That's why we were so helpful in the beginning. We were both trying to hit on you.'

His shy laughter was infectious and Sadie smiled as she remembered how they'd fallen over themselves to be kind. God, she could be naïve.

'But then, we realized we had a problem. Neither of us was getting anywhere and there were a few times when we near came to blows telling the other to get out of the way so one of us could have a clear run at you.'

'Hold on a minute.' Sadie stopped walking. 'Did it occur to either of you to ask if I was even interested?'

'Well, it never really got that far.' Kyle scooped her hand into his. 'As time went on, you just became one of the guys. Gabe and me agreed it was best that way, so we decided to leave well alone.'

'Why didn't you tell me?' she asked. 'I had no idea.'

'What would you have done if we told you?'

She shook her head with a laugh. 'I don't know, but certainly not what I did in the bar the other night.'

'Point is, you did do it and you can't unring a bell, Sadie.' Gabe's voice stayed calm but she could see the grim set of his mouth. 'Things have changed between us now and they can never go back.'

'I know,' she whispered, her face flaming as she felt the tension rise between them again. 'But I'm gonna make it right.'

Sadie groaned inwardly as she saw the hope spring to life in Gabe's eyes. Kyle began to grin as he let out a ragged breath and she realized that she'd said the wrong thing again. 'No. I don't mean that.

I mean, I should leave town.' She put a hand up to silence their protests. 'That way, things will go back to normal.'

'So you're gonna run away? You are simply going to cause this mess and then hightail it out of here.' Gabe took a few steps away from her as if struggling to keep hold of his anger. 'How in God's name do you think that is going to help?'

'W-what else can I do?' Surprised by the sudden change in his mood, Sadie asked the question without thinking. Gabe simply stared at her while Kyle moved to hold her upper arms and turn her his way.

'You know what you can do.'

He was right. She did.

Chapter 5

She watched them quietly from the corner of the small room in the converted outbuilding Gabe lived in, just a few yards from where he worked every day. She remembered Kyle telling her he lived in a similar but larger place nearby that he had to share with a few other guys. He said he hated it, which is why he spent as much time as he could out of the joint.

She clutched the tumbler of whisky Gabe had shoved wordlessly into her hand after they'd walked in. He knocked his back in a single swallow and banged the glass down onto the table. Kyle took a sip of his, grimaced and then forced himself to follow suit. The realization that Kyle pretty much hero-worshipped the other man hit her like a bolt of lightning. Why hadn't she seen it before now?

There was plenty she hadn't seen before. Like just how much they cared for her, or how much she wanted what they'd been offering. She wasn't sure exactly what it was that either of them had said that had changed her mind but they had. As she'd spoken about leaving town, the words had caused her pain, a pain, which had been intensified by their reaction to the idea. Gabe had told her in words of one syllable that he would pretty much hunt her down and drag her ass back to Hurley.

Sadie knew running away would be futile and not just because of Gabe's threat. She could hide from them, but she couldn't hide from her own feelings. She realized that now. So much time had been wasted in fighting them that she'd never stopped to ask herself what she really wanted.

Coming to the apartment meant more than simply joining the guys for a nightcap. Sadie knew what she was agreeing to. And, besides a flutter of nerves regarding how in the hell she could satisfy the both of them at the same time, she was breathless at the idea.

'Look, Sadie,' Gabe began, shaking her out of her reverie. 'I, or rather we, don't want you to do this if you're not ready.'

'Right.' Why in hell was he so nervous? Kyle seemed much more relaxed and she tried to feed off his energy rather than Gabe's. The prospect of what could be about to go down between them made her scared and excited enough already without him making it any worse.

'It's just I don't know any other way to put this behind us and move on,' Gabe continued.

A thought she simply couldn't get out of her head came out of her mouth before she had time to stop it. 'It didn't seem to stop you looking elsewhere the other night.'

'What do you mean?' Kyle asked.

'That brunette I overheard you two discussing. No, it's not jealousy if that's what you are thinking,' she added quickly when she saw Kyle laugh and Gabe roll his eyes. 'You sure looked ready to move on to me.'

'We were still mad as hell and knew you could hear whatever we said,' Kyle admitted, his face reddening. 'It seemed like a good idea at the time.'

'Well, I sure know how that feels,' she said, wincing at the memory. Her heart thumped when she realized that speaking about her little performance caused a different reaction in the men. Gabe stopped pacing to stare at her wordlessly. Kyle grabbed the whisky and refilled his glass, then did a better job of swallowing it down in one gulp than he had the first time. Sadie couldn't help but laugh when he still made the same comical face.

'I don't know what in the hell you think is so funny.' Gabe's irritation surprised her. 'Sorry,' he said almost instantly, removing his hat and throwing it onto a seat.

'Calm down,' Kyle warned him.

Gabe looked at her again. 'Maybe you'd better go.'

'Why?' Kyle said, saving her from asking the same question.

'Because I couldn't handle it if you changed your mind. I've spent so much time fantasizing about that night and, now you're here, all I want to do is pin you to the wall and ram my cock into you over and over again.' The words came out in an angry rush until he paused for breath, running his hands through his light brown hair as his chest heaved. 'But despite all that, if I can't be sure you are agreeing to this for the right reasons, then I think you'd better leave.'

He sank to the bed, flopping back onto it as he fought to calm himself. Sadie sat in shock, fire coursing through her as she stared at his body until Kyle's words to Gabe reached through her fog.

'Buddy, I feel the same way but you gotta take it easy.' His eyes found hers. 'It's all up to Sadie now.' He kept his composure better than his friend but she didn't doubt his feelings ran as deeply. His body sank back against the counter and his groin got hard under her gaze, as if she'd really touched him. The challenge in his eyes darkened them to an inky black, and she heard a hiss as he sucked in a breath and bit down into his bottom lip while he waited for her to make a move.

Sadie did move, but not in his direction. She shrugged off the jogging suit she wore and got down to her nightshirt before she dared another look at either of them. Kyle's eyes began to glitter possessively, but he wasn't her priority at that moment.

Gabe had her full attention. He seemed to be in torment and she wanted, or rather needed, to make it better. Kyle would take care of himself.

Gabe's body lurched upwards as he felt the first touch of her nails scraping up the denim of his thighs. His shocked expression disappeared as Sadie massaged the powerful muscles beneath her palms, shushing him when he began to speak so she could concentrate on inching nearer and nearer to his penis swelling at the crotch of his jeans.

Sliding over his body to put her full weight on him, Sadie cupped his face in her hands and looked deeply into his eyes before kissing him, so that he would know this was what she wanted. His reaction was all she could hope for. His hands came up to crush her head closer as his hot tongue forced its way between her lips.

Sadie dragged her mouth from his to sit back across his thighs and she tore the shirt from his jeans, ripping open the buttons and dragging it from his shoulders. Job done, her hands dropped to the buckle at his waist and she worked quickly to free his cock. Gabe hissed and lurched forward again as she pulled him free of his clothing. His penis was hard and thick and she felt him jerk as she ran her hand up the length of it, flicking her thumb over the top.

'Baby, slow down,' he gasped, smiling to take the edge off his words.

She laughed, feeling no embarrassment. Her sudden and drastic change of heart had surprised her almost as much as it did Gabe. 'Sorry. I kind of got carried away.'

'Don't you dare apologize,' she heard Kyle say behind her. Sadie turned to find him naked and standing at her side. In her rush to get at Gabe, she hadn't heard him move.

'Take your hat off, idiot.' Kyle didn't take offense at Gabe's words, turning to throw his hat across the room with a silly grin. Gabe took the opportunity to shrug his jeans down his legs and off his feet before pulling her back across his lap.

Kyle leaned forward to grab her nightshirt at the hem and rip it clean up over her head. She felt a moment's shyness as two sets of eyes raced over her skin but forgot it as soon as Kyle pushed her forward over Gabe's body. Sadie held her breath as she felt him spread the cheeks of her ass seconds before his hand slid under her.

Gabe caught her as she flopped forwards, bunching her hair in his hands to hold her mouth against his and force her to take Kyle's touch. She quivered as the man between her thighs slid first one, then two fingers into her tight pussy. Her low, guttural groan was swallowed by Gabe's mouth as Kyle palmed a handful of her leg, spreading her wider as he slid in and out of her again and again.

Her ears zoned in on Gabe's ragged breathing beneath her. Sadie felt the hard ridge of his cock pressing into her abdomen and realized she'd been grinding against it as she rode Kyle's hand. Lifting her body, she allowed just the hard tips of her breasts to touch his skin as she slid back down his torso. Her nipples grazed a path down towards his groin and she closed her eyes, biting her lip against the change in sensations as she moved from the smooth skin on his abdomen to the hair covered muscle of his thighs.

'Ah, fuck,' he groaned as she encased his penis between her breasts for the briefest moment before allowing him what he wanted. Kneeling between his legs, she filled her mouth with the cock that throbbed as her lips closed over it and she tasted the saltiness of his arousal.

Kyle moved with her, dropping to his knees on the floor behind her position at the edge of the bed and spreading her legs wide. His fingers dipped inside her again before he slid the flat of his hand forwards over her clit. His movements were slow and sensual, teasing the first tentative spasms from her. But as she began to groan loudly around Gabe's cock, his touch got bolder. Soon, Kyle's hand began rubbing her fast and hard and Sadie had no choice but to tear her mouth from Gabe as a sudden and violent orgasm ripped through her. Kyle bunched her hair in his free hand and forced her head back as if he wanted to see her face as she came.

As she shook and quivered between them, she felt Gabe cup her breasts, flicking his thumbs over her nipples as his low, seductive voice washed over her. 'God, you are so beautiful, baby,' he whispered over and over.

'Stop…stop,' she pleaded breathlessly as her climax passed and her skin became hypersensitive to Kyle's touch. He complied immediately, getting to his feet behind her and smoothing a caressing hand over her butt.

Sadie focused again on her goal of overwhelming Gabe the way Kyle had just done to her. His cock throbbed in her hand as she tugged on it and her eyes drank in the sight of the big, gorgeous man writhing beneath her touch. She saw his eyes flick above her head and his almost imperceptible nod to the man standing over them. Sadie realized what had passed between them as she heard Kyle rip open a foil packet and then felt the first push of his dick teasing its way inside her.

Any question she had about what it meant was chased from her mind by Kyle's body. His penis felt long and hard and his deep probing brought tears to her eyes. His strokes were slow and measured and he seemed to enjoy pushing in as far as he could if his ragged cries were anything to go by. His gentle lovemaking surprised Sadie, as did his sudden, intense orgasm. His fingers bit into her skin, and he impaled himself deep inside her with one last thrust as he gave a long, low groan in the back of his throat.

Kyle fell back immediately, sinking to his knees. 'You ok?' Sadie asked when he disappeared out of view. A breathless grunt in reply was her only clue as to where he'd fallen to recover.

Gabe put an end to any further conversation by making it clear he'd been waiting for Kyle to get the hell out of the way. 'At last,' she heard him mutter under his breath, moments before he lifted her bodily to pin her beneath him on the mattress.

Sadie lay beneath him, happy at his impatience to have her. His mouth locked over hers, nibbling and sucking at her lips as one of his hands made its way between her thighs. She jumped at his touch, taking a moment to adjust to his firm pressure against her clit.

'Where are you going?' she asked urgently as she felt him move.

'I want to taste you, baby,' he said as he slid away from her. 'The thought of having my mouth on your pussy has been driving me crazy for days.' He parted her to his gaze and chuckled low in his throat as her body convulsed inches from his face.

'Gabe…please,' she groaned. Why was he waiting? Couldn't he see how much she wanted him?

'Do you know how hot it is to see you quiver like that while you wait for me to touch you?' Sadie felt her body pulse again at his words, and she knew from his low laugh that he'd seen her reaction to his words. She held her breath, determined not to beg him but praying he wouldn't wait much longer.

Finally—blessedly—he dipped his head. The gentle lapping at the entrance to her pussy surprised Sadie but it wasn't what she wanted. She vocalized her frustration with a low groan as she squirmed against him, trying to bring his attention up to where she needed it. Gabe took the hint, moving his mouth immediately and sucking her clit between his lips.

Her body cleared the bed as the first, intense spasm rocketed through her. As if Gabe knew he'd discovered what she needed, he grappled her ass into his palms and locked his mouth over her. His touch felt firm to the point of being rough but to Sadie, it couldn't have felt better. In what seemed like no time at all, her hands had knotted into his hair and she forced him to stay still as she ground her orgasm out against his face.

Gabe pulled away as soon as she had finished, but the moment to compose herself didn't last long. Pausing only to put on a condom, he moved over her instantly, holding her legs wide apart with a strong hand at the back of each knee. Unlike Kyle, Gabe didn't poke tentatively at her entrance as if asking permission to enter. He simply held her body still as his gaze locked with hers and forced his thick cock inside her. He took in her every reaction and Sadie saw the glimmer of satisfaction in his eyes when she gasped as he filled her to the hilt.

Dropping her legs, he supported his weight on his palms to lay over her. Locking his mouth on hers again, his tongue mimicked the actions of his cock as both plundered in and out of her. Sadie tore her mouth away to moan as she took Gabe's first, full thrust. He was everything Kyle was not—rough, demanding and overwhelming. She clung on blindly, overpowered by his intensity. Every time he slammed into her, she groaned loudly as a new level of pleasure raced through her and it seemed to spur him on. She closed her eyes against the onslaught, only to hear him whisper in her ear.

'Look at me, Sadie. I want you to know who it is fucking you like this.' His voice sounded hot and loaded with possession, and confusing given the circumstances.

'It's Gabe,' she whispered back, smiling into his eyes, doing all she could to give him what he needed. His reaction to her words came suddenly and violently as his hands locked onto her hips and he lifted her from the bed to pummel her blindly.

'Oh fuck. Fuck,' he repeated over and over as he spilled into her. His brow knit into a hard line as his eyes clouded over and she watched his face contort into an almost pained expression as the last of his orgasm shuddered through him.

Gabe fell away from her instantly, pausing only to drag the blanket across her body to cover her before collapsing beside her. Kyle, who Sadie guessed had decided to stay out of the way until she and Gabe had finished, appeared at the side of the bed and began donning his clothes.

Gabe rolled off the bed almost instantly, gathering his things quickly and gesturing to Kyle that they should leave the room. 'We'll give you a minute to get dressed, ok?'

Sadie nodded silently, uncertain what to do next. As if sensing her nervousness, both men dropped their heads for a kiss before leaving. 'If it were up to me, I wouldn't let you out of this bed, but we better not let Adie find you here in the morning,' Gabe said with a smile as he backed away. 'Now get your ass up before I change my mind.'

She thought about ignoring his warning and staying right where she was but then the image of Adie bellowing at her spurred her into action. Her boss never usually needed a good reason to chew her ass out over something and she sure as hell didn't intend to give him one!

Chapter 6

Any fear she had that things would be weird afterwards evaporated within a few hours. Sadie was surprised and pleased the next day when Kyle searched her out and invited her to help with his preparation for the show. He wouldn't let her near the bull but made a point of explaining everything he did and the reason for it.

Gabe's attitude pretty much remained the same, except he now thought Kyle as crazy as she. 'If Sadie gets hurt, it's your ass I'm gonna be looking for,' he warned Kyle when he found the pair of them sitting on fence that ran around the bull pen, discussing rope holds.

'Stop worrying. He's being totally overprotective.' Sadie rolled her eyes at Kyle. 'In fact, I'm wondering what the point of it all is if he makes me stand so far away I can barely hear him.'

'That's well and good, but don't forget what I said.' His message to Kyle was clear. The other man's face hardened for a brief second and Sadie feared there could be trouble but as soon as it appeared, Kyle chased his anger away with a shrug.

'Why don't you let me buy you both a drink tonight?' she said quickly, determined to keep them distracted from the topic in hand. She was gonna have to rethink her idea of getting them to teach her. Sadie didn't even know if the friendship between the three of them would survive the aftermath of the night they'd spent together, never mind throwing more fuel onto the fire by giving the guys something to fall out over.

It didn't look like either of them planned to say a word about what happened anyway, she thought later that night as they all settled into a booth with a beer after work. Sadie didn't understand why she felt so at ease the morning after and still did now. She'd fucked the pair of them less than 24 hours earlier yet they were all sitting together, just like the old days as if nothing had changed.

Ok, so she doubted she would ever have another night like that in her life, but she didn't regret it. Not for one second. Individually, Kyle and Gabe could have overwhelmed her in bed, but to have both of them totally focused on her body and driving her crazy together had changed her forever. Sadie had always known she had stronger desires than most guys could handle, but she didn't really know what they were. Not until that night.

She realized she had no idea how they felt about it all. Maybe one of them regretted it or they'd agreed between them never to go there again. The thought circled in her head, changing shape and taking on new meaning until she was forced to blurt out a question. 'So, is anybody gonna mention it or are we just supposed to pretend it never happened?'

'Well, that's kind of up to you,' Gabe said carefully. His face gave no clue as to his feelings about it. Kyle was a little easier to read. His eyes lit up with hope at the mention. It didn't take a mind reader to figure out what he wanted. Sadie's attention returned to the silent and enigmatic Gabe.

'Why is it always up to me?' His attitude began to piss her off. Would it kill him to tell her that he'd enjoyed it as much as she had and that he wanted more of the same? 'Seems to me I have to make all the decisions around here.'

'What the hell is that supposed to mean?'

'You know exactly what I mean. To hear you tell it, it was my fault you and Kyle even confessed your little game and that you two have so little self control that I was able to turn you on so easily. Then, you had the nerve to tell me that it's my fault you couldn't get it out of your head afterwards.'

'It might have sounded that way but that's not what we meant, and you know it.' Gabe's eyes had gone a cold, stormy green. Despite the warning in his tense face, it pleased her to see she'd at least gotten a reaction out of him.

'Now, you sit here like nothing has changed.' She laughed in self derision. 'But I guess for you guys, nothing has. I'm not the first woman you've had together and I'm sure I won't be the last.'

To her fury, his face relaxed into a knowing smile and he wore the look of a man who had it all figured out. 'Tell me what you want me to say.'

'I don't want to have to tell you,' she shouted, before lowering her voice as she realized she'd been making a scene. 'I don't know what I want but I sure as hell don't want you sitting here acting as if it's no big deal. It was one hell of a big deal to me.'

'Have I said that?' His smile had slipped and he leaned forward, his face inches from hers as he stared into the depths of her eyes.

'No, but that's just the problem. You haven't said anything.'

For some reason, Kyle got a look from Gabe that could strip paint from the side of a barn. 'And I suppose he has, right?'

'Hey, don't drag me into this, I haven't said a thing.' Despite her irritation, Sadie gave Kyle a small grin to show him it wasn't his fault she got angry. True, he hadn't said anything either but his attitude towards her had changed. He treated her like she was special at least, which was more than could be said for his friend.

Gabe seemed confused. 'So, what's the difference?'

'Forget it,' she muttered, unsure herself what she was really asking for.

'What do you want from me?' he persisted. He leaned closer, dropping his voice to barely more than a low rumble. 'You want to know how I feel, is that it?' Sadie nodded, hypnotized by the heat in his eyes and voice.

'Well it ain't gonna happen here,' he said, shocking her out of the seductive haze she'd been about to slip into. She gasped in outrage before she saw that look that passed between the two men. 'There's something you gotta understand, Sadie. There's no way in hell I am gonna sit here and get all touchy feely in front of a buddy, no matter who he is. No offense, Kyle,' he said, turning his attention to the other man.

'None taken,' Kyle said, laughing as they clinked their beer bottles together.

'Well, I'm sure as hell offended,' she ground out through gritted teeth. 'Are you guys seriously telling me that you can have sex with me together, but you can't talk about your feelings in front of each other?'

'Damn straight,' Kyle said, his open, honest expression draining the anger from her. Gabe nodded to confirm what his friend had said, leaving Sadie to stare at them both in bemusement.

'You ok?' Gabe asked a few minutes later. 'You've gone awful quiet.'

'Just tired I guess.' Truthfully, she'd gotten tired of thinking. Her brain had been racing since their conversation had ended and she had no idea what she thought about anything anymore.

'Let me visit the men's room, and then we'll walk you home,' Kyle said, getting up from the table.

Gabe turned his head and watched him walk away, before swinging around and leaning towards her across the table. 'Ok, now we can talk. What do you want me to say?'

'I don't know,' she stammered, taken aback by his sudden return to their earlier conversation.

'I'm not much good with words, Sadie, but I can tell you that what happened was a big deal for me, too.' The warm, husky tones that had seduced her so easily were back in his voice and she felt herself slipping into the sound as his words washed over her. 'Would it help you to know that I've barely thought of anything else since it happened and that whenever I close my eyes, asleep or awake, all I can see is you?'

'That helps,' she said, blushing as a smile she couldn't suppress split her face.

'And that every minute, I want to drag you back to that bed and fuck you for the first time all over again. Next time, I won't stop until I make you cry and scream my name as you come from just the feel of me inside you.'

'Shit,' she whispered, the breath torn from her lungs at the heat in his gaze and the pulsing of her body. She squirmed against the pressure building in her pussy, feeling it quiver as she saw him notice her reaction to his words.

'You said it.' Gabe smiled tightly as he watched Kyle return. 'So don't push me about it in front of him again, ok?'

'Sorry,' she said. But she wasn't sorry, she was thrilled.

Her exhilaration at Gabe's words hadn't lasted long. The guys had walked her to her door and then left her there with nothing more than a chaste kiss on the cheek.

When she made it into the stables the next morning, the horses gave her wary glances, unsettled by her strange mood. 'I'm not mad at you, guys,' she said to them all, determined not to rattle the sensitive animals.

She worked quietly and efficiently, getting everything done way quicker than she needed to due to the irritation speeding her arm. Sadie took her lunch pail into the back of the stable and sank down behind a stall, wiping the sweat from her face with a dirty rag from her pocket.

'Sadie?' she heard Gabe call, moments before his face appeared over the wooden frame. 'What you doing there?'

'Just eating lunch,' she said as casually as she could, considering that her stomach had just flipped a dozen times.

'Well, come on, we haven't got all day.'

'For what?'

Gabe's face turned away and she saw a nerve tick in his jaw. 'Do you want to learn how to ride a bronco or not?' He walked off, expecting her to follow blindly. Sadie was so taken back by his change in attitude that she leapt to her feet without question and raced to catch up to him.

'Huh,' he grunted with a smile as he saw her fall into step beside him.

'What made you change your mind?' she asked, out of breath as she struggled to keep up with his long strides.

'No questions, ok? Just listen and learn.'

With that, he launched into a long and complex explanation of the rules. Much of it Sadie already knew, but she dared not tell him. He started with saddled bronco.

'Saddle up carefully while the horse is in the chute and pull the cinch tight. You gotta grasp the reins with one hand—that's obvious—but you can't touch either the horse or yourself with your free hand.'

'Ok.' She nodded, keen to show her understanding and encourage him to keep going.

'We use something called dry rosin to help keep a grip on the rope. You can be disqualified for using anything else. Same with changing hands on the rein or wrap it around your hand, pulling leather or losing a stirrup.'

An hour later, she got antsy. Gabe had droned on and on about the rules, the saddles, the reins, everything in fact except the damn horses. She cleared her throat, nervous to bring the subject up but compelled to all the same. 'So, when do I get to ride one?'

'What? A bronco? Can't see it happening any time soon,' he said, turning back to his demonstration of how to cinch the rigging.

'Why not?' Her heart sank to her boots.

'Use your head, Sadie. You asked me to teach you how to ride a bronco, and I am. I can't do anything about the horses though. I'm sure as hell not going to risk my job or your neck by putting you on one.' He held a hand up to her protest. 'Do you realize how much money you'd cost Adie if an uninsured rider damaged some of his precious stock?'

'Then what's the point?' she said, throwing her hat onto a bale of hay in frustration.

Gabe picked it up for her, putting it back on her head and brushing away a smudge from the dirty cloth she'd used earlier on her chin. 'The point is if Adie ever decides to put you on the payroll as a rider, then you're insured and both our asses are covered.'

'I guess.' She sighed, unhappy with what he'd said but unable to disagree with the logic. As usual, the bigger implications of getting what she wanted hadn't occurred to her. Other people's livelihoods and reputations were at stake, not just her own ambitions. Sadie hadn't thought of that when she'd pushed Gabe, Kyle and even Billy into helping her.

Still, it was Adie's fault for luring her into the job under false pretenses. 'Seems to me like neither of you were completely honest,' Gabe reminded her when she spoke her mind.

Sadie pouted a little longer. He seemed determined to make her see the bright side of the situation and he'd thrown an arm around her shoulders to drag her into a hug, trying to cheer her up. 'Hey, what are you doing later?'

'Not riding a bronco, that's for sure. Why do you ask?'

'Kyle and me have been invited to a party over at the Mayor's place. He reckons the local news will be there. He's trying to attract more tourism to the town and figures having a couple of the guys from the rodeo is a good idea.'

Sadie shook her head. 'I don't know, Gabe. What will I wear? God, I haven't been to a formal party in years.'

'Don't worry too much. He wants the guys to wear western attire, obviously. Just throw on a dress.' He stopped walking to turn her in his arms. 'You do have a dress, don't you?'

She elbowed him in the ribs. 'Of course I have a dress. What I don't have is time to take a bath, do my hair, buy some pantyhose—'

'Ok, ok. I get the message.' Gabe raised his hands in mock surrender. 'Would it helped if I talked Adie into letting you have the rest of the day off?'

'I'd be very grateful,' she said, letting her voice load the words with unspoken promise.

'How grateful?' His hands dropped to her hips as he took a step closer. A tingle raced up her abdomen as the hard ridge of his sudden erection brushed against her.

'Very.'

Sadie watched a thought cross his face, the darkening of his eyes making it clear that it had been a dirty one. Gabe had just begun to lower his mouth towards hers when Adie turned the bend. Thankfully, the boss was deep in conversation on his cell and didn't spot them until Gabe had taken a reluctant step away. 'You better make yourself scarce,' he muttered. 'We'll pick you up at eight, ok?'

She backed away, grinning at the sight of him trying to cover his arousal with his hat. Gabe's rueful smile warned her he'd make her pay for it later.

Chapter 7

'Wow!'

Sadie couldn't think of anything else to say as the limo slowed down to a crawl on the gravel drive in front of the grandest house she had ever seen. Ok, maybe not the grandest she'd seen but certainly the most impressive she had ever been in or probably would be again.

The Mayor's residence was owned by the town and on the National Register of Historic Places. The Victorian mansion, built at the turn of the century, had just under 30 rooms spread over its 3 floors. To Sadie's eyes it looked like a miniature version of The White House, adorned as it was with balconies, balustrades and columns.

'You can say that again,' Kyle said as the three of them got out of the car.

'You didn't tell me the place looked like this,' she admonished Gabe, looking down at her simple blue cocktail dress in despair. 'I knew I should have gone out and bought something new.'

Both men stopped their progress up towards an open front door with noise and light spilling out of it. 'You're kidding, right?' Gabe seemed surprised by her words.

'Sadie, you are gonna be the best looking woman there,' Kyle added, running down the few steps separating them and grabbing her hand to pull her forwards. 'You couldn't have picked anything better.'

'He's right,' Gabe whispered as they approached the door. 'That dress is hot. You look amazing and since I saw you in it, my mind hasn't stopped working on ways to get you out of it.'

'Amen to that,' Kyle said, running the most casual of caresses across the small of her naked back, sending shivers down her spine.

Sadie basked in their approval and the knowledge of how hot they seemed to be for her even as she suspected that they were just being kind.

The dress was a backless halter style with a V neck that she'd complemented with a silver choker. The full skirt ended just below the knee and had been cut on the bias, making the fabric swish around her legs as she moved. The satin dress, the color of bright sapphires, turned her eyes a deeper shade of blue, which was the reason she'd bought it a few years back. Tonight was its debut and she felt thrilled by the reaction she'd gotten so far. Despite her nervousness, she realized she didn't really care what anybody else thought. When she'd chosen to leave her hair loose around her shoulders save for diamante comb holding it back over one ear, she'd been dressing to please them.

Regardless of whom it was she'd made the effort for, many of the men in the room stopped talking to stare at her boldly as she entered. Kyle seemed to find the whole thing very amusing, but Gabe wasn't impressed. She felt a possessive hand at her back as he forced them in turn to look away with a dead-eyed stare.

Thankfully for all involved, the Mayor seemed to be a friendly, old man with nothing but kindness in his gaze and a laugh in his voice. 'Glad you and your lovely lady friend could make it, boys. Come in and make yourselves at home. Martha,' he yelled in the general direction of the housekeeper, 'bring these young people a drink.'

Sadie took the offered champagne eagerly, relieved to have a reason to extricate her fingers from the Mayor's exuberant handshake. As soon as was polite, she took a step back to allow the guys to do what they'd been invited for—talking up the rodeo, and therefore the town.

Casting a look in their direction 30 minutes later, she decided she'd had enough of deflecting the lewd glances of the husbands present and the 'drop dead, bitch' glares from some of their wives.

She'd got it wrong again. Sadie groaned internally. She'd been so worried about impressing the men she'd gone on a date with that she turned a perfectly respectable dress into an invitation for all to leer at her.

A visit to the ladies room gave her a welcome break from the tension. Sadie decided to use it as an excuse to explore. Many people milled around the hallways and vast rooms, admiring the art adorning the walls. She found herself alone in what looked to be a small library dominated by a large oil painting over the fireplace. The striking image depicted a bull carrying a fallen rider to a hillside grave and brought tears to her eyes. The way the broken body of the cowboy had been laid Christ-like across the animal's horns evoked thoughts of the sacrifice he'd been prepared to make. The bull bore his burden proudly, as if honoring the man and the final battle he had lost. The sadness and nobility of the scene touched Sadie deeply and told her two things. First, that the Mayor really did love the rodeo and second that she probably wasn't brave enough to risk her life so easily night after night.

A giggle from the hallway caused her to turn moments before Kyle backed through the open doorway, dragging a smiling young woman in behind him. Frozen to the spot, Sadie didn't know what to do as she saw him tilt his head, preparing to kiss the girl. She cleared her throat loudly, causing the couple to jump and spin in her direction.

Kyle's face lost a little color as he saw her and he took a slow, measured step away from his playmate. 'Sadie…we were looking for you.'

'Oh, and you thought I was hiding down her throat?' She couldn't help but tease him. He bore the look of a man with his hand caught in the cookie jar. Her easy laughter chased some of the tension out of his face and he smiled sheepishly, taking off his hat and scratching his head in confusion.

He wasn't the only one feeling confused Sadie realized as she made her excuses and left them alone. Why didn't it bother her more that Kyle had arrived with her but was chasing other women? Her previous reaction to the idea of him and Gabe turning their devastating charms on someone else had made her insane with jealousy less than a week ago, so what had changed? If anything, she should care more now, not less.

Gabe seemed to be genuinely looking for her when she found him again in the lobby. 'There you are. I was beginning to worry that one of these dirty old dogs had you pinned in a corner somewhere.'

She laughed. 'Don't worry about me, I can handle myself.'

The appraising look he gave her in reply carried a lot of heat. 'Oh, I know you can.' What was it with those damned green eyes of his? He merely had to turn them on her while using that husky, deep voice and she wanted to fling herself at his feet. Sadie was grateful he had no real idea just how much he affected her.

She stayed by his side for the next hour, watching quietly as he shook about a million hands, posed for some photos, gave his autograph to a few people and had an interview with a totally infatuated local news reporter.

'So, you all done being a celebrity?' she asked when they finally found a quiet corner to retreat to.

'I guess so.' A spot of color on his cheeks told her that being the focus of so much attention hadn't been easy for him. 'Kyle's better at this kind of thing than me. Where is he by the way?'

'Last time I saw him, he had some pretty young thing in his sights.'

'Kyle's with a girl?' Sadie nodded, taking a sip of her champagne as Gabe's quiet study of her reaction made her feel self conscious. 'Don't you mind?'

'Why should I? What he does is none of my business.'

'Right,' he said, some of the warmth leaving his gaze. 'Talk of the devil, here he is.'

Kyle approached with his hands held out in surrender. 'Sorry about that, Sadie. Some of these girls are crazy. She wouldn't leave me alone.'

'Yeah, I could see you were putting up a real fight,' she drawled, rolling her eyes at Gabe, sharing her joke with him in an effort to make him smile again. His face had set into a stony mask and she had no idea why.

'You know I'm saving myself for you,' Kyle murmured into her ear, brushing a tendril of hair out of his way to place a kiss on the curve of her shoulder. 'I've been waiting all night to—'

'Let's just get out of here,' Gabe said, dragging his eyes away from her nipples as they reacted to Kyle's nearness. He headed for the door, stopping impatiently and grabbing her hand as she got level with him.

'What's the rush?' she said, minutes later after she'd been propelled less than gently into the backseat. Sadie found herself sandwiched between two men radiating very different, but no less intense energies.

'I couldn't breathe in there, that's all.' Gabe would say no more, taking off his hat and opening the window to take a deep, cleansing breath.

His brown hair fluttered against his brow over his closed eyes and Sadie wondered what had him so tense. She placed a hand on his forearm to drag his attention back to her. 'You ok?' He paused and then turned to her, his expression much calmer than it had been minutes earlier.

'I'm fine, sweetheart.' The endearment made her smile and he returned it with one of his own, brushing away the tendril of hair blown across her cheek by the breeze rushing in through the open window. His eyes roamed over her face before continuing down, passed her shoulders, to the place where her breasts were crushed against his bicep. Sadie's nipples drew his attention and a small smile lifted the corner of his mouth. 'Are you cold?'

She shook her head, staring boldly into his face. The fluttering in her pussy intensified into a deep, hungry ache as his gaze dropped back down to her breasts and he sucked in a loud breath. Gabe lifted her hand from his forearm and placed it on the hard bulge in his jeans. Her eyes flew back to his and he laughed at her shocked expression. 'Why are you so surprised? I told you that dress is hot.'

Gentle knuckles brushing across the underside of her ass from Kyle's side of the limo forced her to move back towards the middle of the seat. Sadie crossed her legs, placing her purse on her lap and her hands on top of it. One of them had to show some restraint and it looked like it would have to be her.

'If you guys don't start behaving yourself, we're gonna be the talk of the town.'

Chapter 8

Sadie's first orgasm of the night came suddenly and without warning. Stripped down to her thong within minutes of walking into Gabe's place, she'd been thrown onto the bed and had to endure the sight of them ripping off their own clothes. Side by side, the differences in their physiques were easier to see. Kyle's compact body seemed darker, partly due to his coloring but mostly due to the small thatches of shiny black hair at his chest and groin. Gabe's muscles were long and finely honed and although he actually had more body hair than Kyle, it was a fine, light brown that caught the light and made the skin on his thighs and forearms glow.

Kyle moved to join her on the bed but Gabe had held him back with a firm hand on his shoulder. 'Tell us what you want,' he said.

'You two, here on the bed with me now.'

Gabe ignored her answer. 'What do you want?' Her face flamed as she realized what he'd asked her. He spared her any further blushes by reaching forward and grasping her ankles in a firm hand, pulling them apart to make space for his body. 'Fuck, you're so wet,' he gasped as he looked at the place where her panties clung to her folds.

Kyle kneeled on the edge of the bed beside her hips, leaning over to run a finger through the moist crease.

'No,' Gabe said. Kyle stopped, giving the other man a quizzical look. 'I want to see her do it.'

'Yeah, that's it. Touch yourself, baby,' Kyle said as he dragged her hand down and pressed it against her pussy. Sadie jumped at the pressure, a wave of moist heat pulsing from her and chasing away her embarrassment. She closed her eyes and used her free hand to pull her thong to one side, exposing herself to their eyes. Gabe's hands slid silently up to her thighs and he pulled her legs further apart, causing another spasm to race through her.

'Jesus,' Kyle gasped, 'you like us watching, don't you?'

Sadie listened for Gabe's reaction but he stayed quiet, forcing her to look at him through the slits of her eyes. He appeared rigid with fascination, staring at her body so intensely that she could almost feel his gaze on her. She slid her fingers down to her pussy, plunging them inside once and then using them to lubricate her clit. Kyle reached over and snapped the thin straps of her thong before dragging it out of the way, allowing them both a better view. A tremor shuddered down Gabe's torso as she dipped her hand again and he bit down on his lip as if to hold back the groan that rumbled from his chest anyway. Sadie slammed into her orgasm instantly, her gaze filled by the vision of the naked and breathless cowboy who seemed shaken to the core by the mere sight of her.

The almost unbearably intense climax made her want to close her legs around her hand but she couldn't. Gabe's grip on her thighs remained firm and she struggled against it as the spasms forced her body from the bed time and time again.

He let her go as she came back down to earth and she flopped back against the bed to pant loudly. 'Fuck,' was all she could say, followed by a throaty laugh. Gabe smiled down at her, seeming happy to wait until she caught her breath. Kyle had other ideas, scooting to the top of the bed and leaning over her for a kiss before turning her face towards his burgeoning cock.

Sadie got on all fours, happy to please the impatient cowboy yes, but also to tempt the still passive Gabe into action. She opened her mouth to allow Kyle in, flicking her tongue over the salty head of his penis and groaning in satisfaction as she felt Gabe's hands grazing over her ass as he approached her. His palms spread and he dropped his thumbs down to part her thighs, causing Sadie to still for a moment and hold her breath as she waited for him.

His entry was smooth and penetrating, her already moist walls allowing him in easily and deeply. Sadie wished she could see the expression on his face as he used his weight to slide his wide length into her until his hips met her thighs. Sure he must be as deep as he could get, she gasped in surprise as he thrust hard and forced his way even farther in.

Kyle began to thrust gently in and out of her mouth and she used her hand clasped around his shaft to control the depth and speed of his actions. His hands bunched in her hair and she could feel his body beginning to jerk erratically, warning her he was about to come. Gabe slowed down, rocking gently into her while she focused on Kyle.

'Oh god, that's good,' he groaned, as Sadie moved her head away and began to pump him furiously with her hand. She turned the attention of her mouth to his thighs, licking and biting his trembling skin. He came in a gush, coating her hand in hot semen as it pulsed out of him. He stilled her fist as his orgasm ebbed away, gasping for breath while he swayed gently on his knees above her. Kyle grasped her chin in his palm and he dropped a kiss on the top of her head before crawling away.

Gabe brought her attention straight back to him as he clasped her hips, pulling her onto his dick and adjusting his position. She felt his hands slide up her torso as his weight moved over her. He cupped her breasts, rolling her aching nipples between his fingers before moving on to caress her shoulders. Bunching her hair in one hand, he grazed the skin on her neck with his teeth before whispering in her ear. 'I'm gonna make you come so hard.'

Using her hair to pull her head back gently but firmly, he put his free hand under her body and between her legs, forcing them farther apart with his own. His thick fingers circled her clit in slow, measured strokes until she began to cry out and push back onto his cock, asking for more. Gabe adjusted his grip on her hair, pulling her almost upright and increasing the movement of his hand, rubbing her briskly as his thrusts intensified.

Sadie braced her weight on her thighs and pushed back against him. 'Gabe,' she cried out as she began to come around his dick and onto his hand. He let go of her hair to clutch at her breast, using it to hold her fast against him as he forced her to ride out her orgasm the way he wanted her to—hard and fast. She thrashed against him, calling his name over and over until wordless shudders wracked her body and she slumped in his arms, spent and exhausted.

Gabe pushed her forwards to the mattress, using the flat of his palm in the small of her back to pin her down. Two or three brutal thrusts were all it took before he followed her climax with his own. His sudden incoherent shouts echoed off the walls and Sadie felt every bit of his orgasm as he jerked and shook against her skin. He dropped onto hands he braced on either side of her body, his forehead resting on her shoulder as he struggled to regain his breath.

Sadie felt him sink down onto the bed beside her as she lay down and the deep, even breathing that followed within minutes told her he'd fallen asleep. Craning her head around to look for Kyle, she found him in the same condition, slumped across the pillows at the top of the bed.

Inching carefully away, she grabbed her clothing and Gabe's shirt to use as a jacket. She dressed in the bathroom before slipping out through the door and walking the short distance home.

Chapter 9

Sadie dragged herself into her apartment the following night, exhausted after a tough day at work. She'd seen Kyle and Gabe only in passing. Kyle had been his usual happy-go-lucky self but Gabe had gone back to his old, wary ways. His mood swings were beginning to piss her off.

She felt a little more human after a long soak in the tub and had just crawled into bed when she heard a gentle tap at her door.

'Were you asleep?' Kyle said, pausing when he noticed what she wore. 'Isn't that Gabe's shirt?'

Sadie dropped her head to hide her embarrassment. 'I borrowed it last night to throw on over my dress. It was getting cold.'

'Why did you take off like that?' Kyle settled down onto the sofa, taking off his hat and boots and making it clear he planned on staying for the time being.

She smiled, despite her irritation at his assumption that he could just roll up anytime he liked. 'We agreed, remember? It's not a good idea for Adie to find us in bed together.'

'It's a worse one for him to find Gabe and me naked and alone in the same bed.' Sadie joined him in his laughter, clapping her hand over her mouth at the thought. 'Don't worry, I woke up early and made it back to my place before dawn.'

'Glad to hear it.' Sadie looked around, hoping Kyle got the hint that she didn't really want him there. 'Look, don't think I am being rude but did you want to see me about something in particular? It's just I was gonna turn in early.'

Disappointment marred his handsome face for as long as it took him to pick his hat up from the coffee table. By the time he turned to her again, the cocky self assurance was back. 'It's nothing. I just had fun last night, is all. And I wondered what you were doing this evening.'

'Sleeping hopefully,' she said, smiling despite herself. Sadie didn't like him treating her like some kind of booty call. It had to be the only explanation for his appearance at such a late hour. 'Didn't you get that girl's number last night? Maybe she's in the mood for some company.'

'You look a little pissed,' Kyle said, getting ready to put his boots back on.

'What gives you the right to just turn up here like this?'

'I just thought, considering what's been going on recently, that you wouldn't mind.'

His words struck a nerve. 'So you think that gives you some kind of rights over me?'

Kyle put his hands up in surrender. 'I never said that, Sadie.'

'You didn't have to.' She stalked to the door and threw it wide open without looking. 'I think you better leave.'

He finished pulling his boots on without feeling the need to rush. Standing finally, his eyes fixed on something in the doorway behind her and he began to smile. Sadie turned to follow the direction of his gaze and found Gabe standing behind her.

'I'd turn right round and head out of here if I were you,' Kyle warned Gabe as he joined him in the open doorway. 'The lady's not in a good mood.'

'I was just telling him that I was about to go to sleep,' she said in a rush, unsure why she actually cared what he thought.

'What are you doing here?' Gabe asked him, ignoring Sadie.

'The same thing as you,' Kyle replied, his expression making it clear he didn't like the other man's tone.

'I doubt it.'

'So, what is it that's so important?' Kyle asked when Gabe continued to stare him down.

'Forget it. ' Gabe's eyes flicked over Sadie, the darkness in them chilling. He looked angrier than she'd ever seen him.

'Do you want to come in while I give you your shirt back at least?' she offered, ignoring Kyle's incredulous expression.

'You can keep it,' Gabe said before walking away to leave them both staring at his retreating back.

'What in the hell is eating him?'

'I don't know, Kyle, but I'm too tired to think about it.' Sadie began to close the door in his face, no longer caring if she seemed rude or not. 'I'll see you tomorrow, ok?'

She rushed to the window overlooking the street, straining her eyes for any sign of Gabe. She saw Kyle step into the street and head back towards the ranch before something made him turn around. Gabe's figure appeared out of a darkened doorway and he approached the other man slowly.

Sadie could see them talking and started to crack open the window to hear what they said but there was no need. Their conversation ended before it had begun. Kyle had placed a hand on the other man's arm in a friendly gesture, just to have it thrown off. Gabe had pushed him away and walked off in the other direction. Kyle stared at him for a second before waving a dismissive hand over his shoulder and heading in the general direction of the bar.

She toyed with the idea of following him to tell him that he was no better than Kyle—turning up unannounced and expecting her to be ready and willing—and to ask him what the hell his problem was. But she doubted she'd get a straight answer from him anyway.

She went back to bed, settling down onto the pillows before allowing herself to analyze what had just taken place. She didn't like Kyle's attitude one bit and, on the surface, Gabe seemed to be suffering from the same assumptions. But for some reason, his appearance at her door didn't make her mad at all. Sadie wished he'd at least hung around long enough to tell her what he wanted. If she was honest with herself she had to admit that he may not have gotten the same reaction as Kyle did, even if he had been after the same thing.

She snuggled farther under the covers, breathing in deeply as the scent from Gabe's shirt reached her nose. Sadie felt glad he'd said she could keep it even though it hadn't been done out of kindness. Her eyes began to close, genuine exhaustion stopping her from thinking more even if she wanted to.

The questions circling in her head like what was up with Gabe and why did she care so much would just have to wait, but things had suddenly gotten really complicated and she didn't know why.

Chapter 10

'What do you mean he's gone?' Sadie snapped, looking around the bar as if expecting to find Gabe hiding in a corner.

'Like I said, he quit.'

'When?'

'A couple of days ago, the morning after we turned up at your place in fact.'

Sadie's mind raced. She hadn't seen him around but it hadn't seemed strange, as she'd been laying low herself. Any hopes she'd had of finding out what had been bugging him had gone.

'Why?' She sank onto a stool and took the beer he put into her hand. 'What made him suddenly up and quit out of the blue like that?'

Kyle shrugged. 'Don't ask me. I'm pretty sure I'd be the last person he'd tell anything to at the moment.'

'I don't believe you.' She got to her feet. 'Fine, don't tell me. I'm getting sick of trying to figure you two out, so if you do speak to him, let him know I said he can kiss my ass.'

'Hold up.' He grabbed her arm to stop her from leaving. 'I'm not lying. I tried asking him why and he looked about ready to rip my head off and said it was none of my damn business.'

Sadie could see he told the truth. 'Ok, then all we gotta figure out now is what you did to piss him off.'

Kyle choked back a laugh. 'Why me? It's just as likely to be you.'

'Me?'

He nodded. 'All I know is, when I tried to talk to him outside your place the other night, he told me to go fuck myself and to stay away from you. By next morning, he'd packed a bag.'

Sadie's heart leapt and then sunk. Gabe's attitude in bed made more sense to her now. For a man who claimed to be happy to share, he'd seemed real possessive, acting as if he couldn't wait for Kyle to get the hell out of the way. But then why, if he did have feelings for her, had he just taken off without explanation?

A thought struck. 'You did tell him nothing happened between us, right?'

Kyle seemed confused. 'No, but I didn't need to. He walked in as you kicked me out.'

'But how would he know how long you'd been in my apartment?' Sadie warmed to her topic. 'I opened the door wearing nothing but his shirt while you put your boots back on.'

'I guess so.' She punched him in the arm. 'Hey, what's that for?'

'When he asked what you'd been doing in my place, you let him think you'd come for the same thing as him.'

'I didn't exactly put him straight, if that's what you mean, but his attitude bugs me. He acts like he owns you,' Kyle explained. 'You know, the morning after the party, he tore a strip off me for flirting with that girl when we were supposed to be with you.'

'But why would he care? I sure as hell didn't. He knew that.'

'He told me I was disrespecting you. I just figured our arrangement was casual, I mean, it's not like we're talking about love, is it?' He began to peel the label from his bottle before Sadie's silence drew his eyes back to hers. 'Is it?'

Her heart thumped loudly in response to his words and she tested the notion out in her head for the first time. It sure would explain a lot. Kyle seemed to make his mind up before she'd even had a chance to think on it.

'Shit, Sadie. Why in hell didn't you say anything?'

She flapped her hands at him, as if swatting away the ridiculous idea. 'Even if it's true, what difference would it have made? Like you said, the two of you were just having fun.'

'That's not what I said exactly.' Kyle seemed to measure his words. 'And besides, I'm only speaking for myself.'

'Thanks,' she joked, desperate for him to stop pushing her on an emotion she'd only just put a name to. 'Glad to know I had such an effect on you.'

'But we're not talking about me,' he said, either missing or just plain ignoring her attempt at humor. 'The more I think about it, I know what the problem is.'

'I wish somebody would tell me,' she said with a shaky smile. Kyle returned it with one of his own and picked her hand up from the bar.

'Come on, Sadie. You can figure it out.' She shook her head, not really rejecting the idea but unsure that the answer could be as simple—or as complicated—as he was suggesting. 'Think about it. He barely let me near you. Hell, he even made me swear that I wouldn't push you too far the first time we all ended up in bed. I had to practically ask permission to f—'

'Ok, ok,' she said to stop him blurting out even more in the middle of the empty room. The girl behind the counter had already cleaned their end of the bar more times than seemed necessary and Sadie could swear she was trying to eavesdrop. But on such a slow night, who could blame her?

Kyle looked around with a smile. 'Sorry,' he said in much a quieter voice. 'It's just that it's all making sense now—how mad he got when he thought I'd been teaching you how to ride and his anger when he found us in your apartment.'

'Maybe to you,' she said, unable to get her head around the drastic change in events. 'To me, it could also mean that he didn't have the stomach for what we were doing. I know I certainly haven't.'

'Really?' Kyle said, something like remorse darkening his face. 'You didn't enjoy it?'

'Are you kidding? It was an amazing experience but it couldn't last. You're right. I can't handle two men at the same time.' She sighed as she realized this mess had been her own doing.

'Oh, I don't know. You seemed more than capable to me.' He smiled and held her gaze, the warm light in his eyes making her blush.

'Sex wasn't the issue. That was the easy part, but I didn't allow for how I was going to feel.'

'About Gabe?'

'About everything,' she said.

Sadie fell silent, lost in her thoughts. An almost painful sensation lodged in her throat as the realization that she'd fucked up again hit her. She only really wanted Gabe. He was the reason she'd been prepared to take on both men, assuming a threesome would be all that was on offer. She felt some guilt as she stared into Kyle's concerned face. He'd been nothing but an extra in a fantasy scenario built from her lust for his friend.

'I gotta go,' she said, getting to her feet. 'I need to think.'

'You need to talk to Gabe,' Kyle replied.

Tears pricked her eyes. 'What's the point?'

'The point is you care about him, and I think he feels the same.'

She picked up her hat, pushing it firmly onto her head as she laughed bitterly at his words. 'Yeah, well if he cared, he'd be here. Gabe doesn't strike me as the kind of guy to run away from what he wants.'

Kyle dropped his eyes, unable to argue with her logic, giving her hand a final squeeze before letting her walk from the bar.

Chapter 11

Sadie trudged home from work one night a couple of weeks after Gabe had disappeared. The days seemed longer and harder for some reason and she blamed the absent cowboy. In fact, she blamed him for most things—from her foul moods to her shattered ambitions—but most of all, for her heavy heart.

She knew none of it had actually been his fault but it seemed far easier not to have to admit that she'd been responsible for her own bone deep sadness. Kyle had done his best over recent days to cheer her up but it hadn't worked. Luckily, he hadn't tried to take their relationship any further realizing almost before she had that she'd fallen in love with Gabe. He'd settled back easily into the role of a friend and, despite her tetchy demeanor with him, she was actually really glad to have him around.

But she couldn't look at him without the image of his friend flashing through her mind and she'd gotten tired of pushing painful thoughts away. She'd given Kyle a bear hug before she left work, saying goodbye although he hadn't known it.

'I'll see you in the morning, sweetheart,' he'd said, brushing a stray hair from her cheek. She'd dropped his gaze, guilt at her deception eating away at her gut. She'd pulled from his embrace without saying anymore, feeling genuinely sad that she would never see him again.

Letting herself into the apartment, she looked around, amazed again at how much stuff she'd managed to accumulate in the few short months she'd been in Hurley. Boxes and bags were piled high, waiting to be loaded into the U-Haul she'd hired for the following day. Trying to leave town without raising anyone's suspicions wasn't easy and she'd been forced to leave everything until the last possible minute.

Sadie scribbled a quick note to her landlady, apologizing for her leaving without giving notice and saying that she hoped a month's rent in lieu of that would be ok. Sealing a check inside, she put the envelope on top of her bag, ready to put it through Mrs. Williams' door with her key in the morning.

By 10pm, with nothing left to do but set her alarm and go to bed, she pulled Gabe's shirt out of a bag, putting it on for the last time. She'd avoided even looking at it for the past couple of weeks but tonight, she would sleep in it. Come morning, it would be one of the things she would leave behind. Sadie saw no point in clinging to something from her past when she'd decided on a clean break and a new start.

A noise in the hall made her sit up in bed a few hours later. It hadn't been that loud and she would never have heard it if she'd actually managed to get to sleep. A creaky board on the stairs confirmed her suspicions that somebody was approaching. With only two apartments in her building, and the certainty that her landlady would never have company in the middle of the night, Sadie held her breath, waiting for a knock at her door.

Maybe Kyle had figured out she'd been up to something? She sure hoped he hadn't misunderstood her reason for clinging onto him so tightly earlier in the day. The last thing she needed right at that moment was to suffer the consequences of another misjudgment on her part.

The gentle tap made her jump despite the fact she expected it. She toyed with the idea of leaving Kyle in the hall but she guessed it didn't matter if he figured out she was leaving. Nothing he could say would change her mind anyway.

But it wasn't Kyle on the other side of the door. It was Gabe.

'Damn, Sadie. Didn't it occur to you to check who it was before you opened the door half naked in the middle of the night?'

His words should have made her angry but they didn't. All she could see was the face—albeit an angry one—of the man she loved. She swallowed down the bubble of excitement that had formed in her throat at his sudden appearance and stepped back wordlessly to allow him in. Sadie warned herself not to read too much into his presence. He could be gone again just as quickly.

'Sorry, I didn't mean to bark at you,' he said, walking in and taking off his hat and leather jacket. He didn't look to be planning on going anywhere soon. Gabe surveyed the room, kicking gently at a box with the tip of his boot. 'So Kyle is right. You are leaving town.'

'Yes, first thing in the morning.' Her voice came out as barely more than a whisper. 'He figured it out, huh?'

'I guess so. He called me about 6 hours ago and told me to stop being such a damn fool and to get my ass back to Hurley.'

'I didn't know he had your number.'

'Neither did I.' Gabe smiled tightly before taking a deep breath and freezing her to the spot with a strange, wary look. 'He told me you've been having a hard time recently.'

'Well, damn,' she said, turning away to hide the tears brought on by the kindness in his eyes. 'You disappeared on me, I mean us. I got worried.'

'Is that all it was, concern for me?'

Sadie knew this could be her only chance to let him know how she felt but he wasn't making it easy. 'No, I missed you, too.'

Gabe pulled his hands out of his back pockets and took a step towards her. 'Kyle seemed to think it was something more.'

She squirmed under his scrutiny. 'What gave him that idea?'

'I don't know. Maybe he knew you slept in my shirt every night?' His half smile tore at her heart.

'It's not every night,' she said, trying to grab onto the humor. Anything was better than his pity. 'You just caught me at a bad time.'

'Damn it, Sadie, why can't you just talk straight?'

'Why can't you?' she fired back.

Gabe ran his hands through his hair, blowing out a loud breath. 'Look, this is coming out all wrong. Let's start again, ok?'

She nodded. 'Do you want a drink? I think I know where I put the coffee.'

'That'd be great. I've been driving for 4 hours straight.'

The butterflies in her stomach went into frenzy. Had he driven all that way just to stop her leaving? The sound of his cell phone ringing in his jacket pocket stopped her asking where he'd been all this time.

'Yes, I'm here,' he said, looking straight at her. Gabe listened to the person on the other end of the line before turning his back on her and muttering a reply. 'Jesus, Kyle, give me a chance. I've only just walked in the door.'

Sadie pretended to search in another box, one that happened to be nearer to Gabe and his intriguing conversation. 'Yes, I'll tell her,' she heard him whisper furiously. 'I said I'll tell her, dammit.'

He snapped the phone shut and got to his feet, coming over to stand above her where she knelt. 'Look, forget the coffee, ok?'

'Don't you need it now?' Her heart sunk. Maybe he just planned to say his piece and leave?

He reached down to grasp her hands and pull her to her feet. 'I need something, Sadie, but it ain't coffee.' His hands moved to her waist, dragging her forward to lean against his body.

'Sex?' she asked, unable to hide the disappointment in her tone. Is that all he'd come for? She tried to pull away but he tightened his grip.

'Dammit, woman, why do you insist on misunderstanding me?' he groaned, resting his forehead against hers.

She smiled as she threaded her hands through his hair to pull his head up so she could look him right in the eyes. 'Misunderstand what exactly? You haven't actually said anything yet.'

His confused frown disappeared as realization dawned. 'I don't reckon I have.' She felt his deep chuckle right through her rib cage and in other places too, places that reacted to the nearness of the man she adored.

'So tell me. What is it you needed so bad that you drove through the night to get it?' Her tone was teasing, her confidence restored by the look on his face and the reaction of his body. 'Tell me, baby. What is it you want?'

'You,' he groaned against her mouth. 'I want you, Sadie.'

She accepted his kiss, unable to resist his insistent mouth. His hands wandered farther down her body, slipping below the edge of his shirt and sliding the fabric up over her ass, exposing her skin to the air. 'I missed you,' she whispered against his hair as his lips made their way across her cheek and down to the curve of her neck.

Gabe groaned against her skin and took a step back to look into her eyes. 'I missed you, too,' he said, dropping her gaze, 'and I love you.'

Her ears barely caught his quietly spoken words but her body got the message loud and clear. He loved her. 'I loved you first,' she said, surprising them both. It wasn't exactly what she meant to say but she'd hate for him to think she felt obliged to say the same.

A rumble of laughter tore from his chest. 'What, is this a competition now?'

Sadie flushed, feeling silly but deciding to bluff it out. 'No, but if it was, I'd be winning.'

'Is that so?' he asked, using his body to force her back towards the bed.

She resisted when she felt the mattress at the back of her knees, dragging his t-shirt out of his jeans and ripping it up over his head. Sadie brushed her thumb over his nipple before dropping down to suck it into her mouth while her hands worked on the buckle of his belt. Her fingertips slid inside the waistband of his boxers, and she sighed when the warm strength of his erection filled her palm. His body shook as she closed her hand around him and he grabbed her hair, pinning her face against his chest.

She sank to her knees, dragging her lips across his skin as she pulled his clothing down around his ankles. His cock danced invitingly in front of her and she didn't hesitate to let him slide into her mouth. She could feel the tension emanating from him and knew he ached to grab her head and force her to hurry but he didn't move except to shudder as she took him to the back of her throat.

Gabe reached down to grasp her arms and drag her back to her feet before pushing her back onto the bed. He sat down beside her to remove his boots and bundled clothing, smiling over his shoulder at Sadie as her hands played across his back.

She sat up and unbuttoned the shirt she wore as he turned around. 'Don't you dare take that off,' he said, crawling across the bed and then reaching over to pull her on top of him. 'Do you know how hard it makes me to see you wearing it?'

'I'm beginning to understand,' she murmured as she straddled him, rubbing her swollen clit along the length of his erection. Her legs shook at the sensation and she closed her eyes, repeating the motion until Gabe's hands forced her hips to stop moving.

'I want to be inside you when I come and it ain't gonna happen if you keep doing that. Get up here and let me kiss you.'

Sliding her body along his, she allowed her full weight to rest on him to take his mouth with her own. Her legs lay either side of his waist and he pulled them farther apart with a strong hand on the back of each thigh.

She tore her mouth from his and gasped as he suddenly and violently impaled her on his cock, moving his hands to her hips to force her to hold still. Sadie pulsed around him, her breath catching in her throat as her eyes began to water from the painfully exquisite sensation.

'I can feel your cunt sucking on me,' he grunted into her shoulder. His body contorted up into hers as he jerked in response every time a spasm rippled through her pussy. Sadie tried to slip a hand down between them to rub her clit but he stopped her.

'I want to come,' she panted against his neck, trying again to free her hand.

'Let me make you,' he whispered, kissing her. She shook her head, about to explain that she'd never had an orgasm that way before, but he began to move inside her while guiding her hips to grind backwards and forwards across his taut stomach. It took her a moment to get the right rhythm but within minutes, she had taken over, bracing herself on her palms to push back onto him.

Gabe began to grunt as her movements became more erratic, his head tossing from side to side as he allowed her to set the pace she needed. Sadie opened her eyes in shock as her orgasm hit hard from out of nowhere and he stilled below her, watching her face as she began to shudder. 'That's it, baby, come all over my cock,' he said, filling his hands with her breasts and flicking his thumbs over her nipples.

'Gabe,' she screamed, closing her eyes as she lost the battle to keep them open. The image seared across her mind was of the expression on his face—one of satisfaction and possession—as if he'd truly claimed her.

He began to move beneath her before the last spasm rippled through her vagina and she bit down on her lip, forcing herself upright to relieve the pressure on her still sensitive skin. His moan of approval sent her farther backwards to brace her weight on his thighs with palms placed behind her back.

Gabe's fingers bit into her hips as he lifted her up and down to bounce on top of him. Sadie marveled at the strength in his arms, watching in fascination as the muscles of his chest, shoulders and biceps tightened into taut, sweat-glistened ridges. A frown creased his handsome face moments before his head lifted and a curse erupted from his throat.

His eyes locked with hers and he opened his mouth as if to speak before another violent spasm rippled through them both and he collapsed back down onto the bed. A lump formed in Sadie's throat as she saw the effect she had on him. His chest heaved as he sucked in one ragged breath after the other.

The difference between his reaction now and when Kyle had been around was immense. She hadn't seen the real Gabe before, not until right at that moment.

'God, I love you so much,' she said, fighting back more tears as she leaned down to kiss him. 'And I'm so glad you came back.'

'Me too, honey,' he said. It was hardly the most romantic thing she'd ever heard but she'd let it slip this time. The poor man could barely draw breath.

Chapter 12

The following day found Sadie leaving town as planned, but she wasn't heading back to Arizona. She left with Gabe, on their way to the ranch he would one day inherit.

'Are you sure your father won't mind my just turning up with you?' She swiveled in the front seat of his pick-up to watch is face carefully for a reaction.

'He might raise an eyebrow, but he won't say much.' Gabe turned to give her a smile. 'My guess is he will be happy that I've found someone I care about enough to bring home. Not that he'd ever admit it.'

Sadie laughed. 'I can see where you get it from now.'

'What?'

'The way you try to hide your feelings.'

'Hmm.' He didn't look pleased at the comparison but didn't argue. 'I got my own place on the edge of the spread anyways so it doesn't much matter what he thinks, although I'm sure he'll love you as much as I do.'

She fell silent for so long that he turned and asked her if she was ok. 'Yes, I'm fine,' she said with a smile. 'It's just scary, you know?'

'Coming home with me?'

Sadie nodded. 'Everything is happening very quickly.'

Gabe shrugged. 'Sure is. But it's not as if we had a lot of time. You were leaving town and I'd already quit. How else are we gonna see each other?'

'But what if this thing between us doesn't lead anywhere?' She felt bad being the one that had to bring it up but they'd been either having sex or asleep since he'd arrived the night before. He'd swept her off her feet with his unexpected appearance and declarations of love. Sadie didn't want to be the one to burst their bubble but they hadn't spent a lot of time really thinking about what they were about to do.

'Then, at least we know we tried. Besides, you're gonna have to look for work and a place to stay anyway. Well now, you can work for me.' He peered at her over his sunglasses, trying to make her smile. 'But I warn you, I'm a slave driver.'

'If I can handle Adie, I think I can handle you.' She slid along the bench seat to place a hand on his thigh.

'Behave yourself,' he warned with a wry smile. 'We got a lot of miles to put behind us before dark.'

His words took her mind back to when he'd first said them and made her think of Kyle. The guy had turned out to be a sweetheart. There would never be anything but a deep friendship between them but she couldn't regret what had happened.

She and Gabe had stopped in to see him on their way out of town to ask a favor and let him know they'd talked. Not that they'd actually done much talking but that was beside the point.

'I'm just glad the pair of you finally saw sense,' he'd said, slapping Gabe on the back. 'What is it you need?'

'Can you take the rental car and U-Haul back for me and tell Adie I'm sorry to skip out on him like this?'

'Sure thing,' he'd said giving her a light hug before turning to Gabe. 'I'll be up for a visit when the season ends.'

'We'll look forward to it,' he had replied, wrapping a possessive arm around her shoulders, a gesture that wasn't missed by Kyle. He'd shaken Gabe's hand and told them to take care of each other before walking away with a wave over his shoulder. She was gonna miss his friendship and easy banter.

'What are you thinking about?' Gabe asked, dragging her mind back to the present.

'The rodeo,' she said, telling him a half truth for the time being. Sadie suspected he'd misunderstand if she revealed her real thoughts.

'I've been thinking about that, too,' he said. 'You don't have to give up on your dream you know.'

Sadie loved him for caring enough to mention it but found it hard to believe. 'Unless you've got a stock ring at home, I don't see I have much choice but to forget about it for now.'

He shook his head. 'But what I do have is access to a few unbroken horses, and what you have is one of the best damn bronco riders in the state to teach you.'

'You'd actually teach me?' She was almost dumbstruck. 'What made you change your mind?'

His shy smile touched her heart. 'I figure if you're brave enough to take a risk on me, then I should do the same for you. If you think you can handle it, I believe you.'

Sadie leaned over to kiss his cheek, a lump in her throat stopping her from telling him how much she loved him. 'But we take it slow, ok? You don't do anything until I say so,' he warned.

'Does that apply in all things?' she asked, her hands beginning to wander down to the apex of his thighs.

He laughed. 'Honey, if we're talking about sex, you feel free to take charge anytime you like.'

'In that case,' she laughed, unzipping his fly and freeing his rapidly swelling cock, 'pull this rig over, Cowboy. I think it's time for my first ride.'

THE END

WWW.LUXIERYDER.COM

ABOUT THE AUTHOR

I live in a beautiful part of the Southwest of England with my fiancé of 15 years and our dog. We have our own small business which allows me to work from home and leaves plenty of free time for my hobbies. My first experience of writing was creating what is known as 'fan fiction' on the Internet forum of one of my favorite artists. Lots of my readers gave me really positive feedback and encouraged me to write more and take things further. Without them, I would never have had the confidence to submit a manuscript. I enjoy the process of writing and creating characters I would like to meet and situations I would love to be in.

Siren Publishing, Inc.

www.SirenPublishing.com

Breinigsville, PA USA
30 December 2009
230030BV00004B/83/P